WATER OF DEATH

Adriana Torres Arreguín

Water of death- Adriana Torres Arreguin.

Original title: Agua de muerte (2020)

To my family,

the one with me and the one who has already left.

MAN

YOU THAT GO AFTER

THE FALLEN CHIMERA,

HERE ENDS

LIFE

AND ETERNITY BEGINS.

Anonymous.

(It is read at the entrance of the museum of

Momias de Guanajuato, in Mexico)

SATIRO

"No one knows what is like, to be the bad man

to be the sad man, behind blue eyes "

The who.

I've been walking through the same block since 10:30 at night. I got so used to the sewer smell of this place that I don't even bother to cover my nose with the silver scarf. The hostility here is felt to the bone. The houses, painted of messages against the Executor, are in darkness, offering a gray landscape. No one in their sanity would dare to show signs of life, not at this time, never in this fraction of *SyanL*, not at this time of year. It is November and the trend always increases at the end, when people feel that there is nothing to lose and everything to leave behind.

The streets of this sector are pure concrete, flat and desert, the few trees that decorate the sidewalks do not have a single hanging leaf and the sound of my footsteps is the only thing that can be heard. In the distance, some ambulance and patrol sirens accompany what in theory, in image, is a beautiful night. And it is, it really is. The warm autumn wind, which is intense in SyanL, moves my hair and it itches in my eyes, which are already irritated and red. I can gaze the SyanL Building of Justice and Courage, standing majestically from the rest. *Sy1* is my city and as a capital, it holds all the important departments of the government of Cesare Tovar, President of the country. His old age is deceptive and his noble face, resembling a wise teacher, with gray beard can make everybody think that he is just an innocent old man.

He is not.

The most recent scandal occurred tonight.

Lito Leggio was killed a few hours ago in an ambush that, as the press reported on official platforms, was planned for many months. Lito had in his possession a shipment of nine wagons of *Joan Megghia* whiskey, the best in the country and my personal favorite. Leggio was in charge of trafficking whiskey in the poor sectors of SyanL, this is precisely one of the neighborhoods in which he operated, without paying any taxes and of course, without giving a single coin as a tribute for the government. Lito was never affected by authority, his face always smiling, did not resemble of a dealer specialized in the pride of our nation: whiskey. He himself drank it very continuously, his oval face, with a half"grown beard, always offered a kind gesture, a protective hand, and a glass of *Joan Megghia.*

They caught him having dinner at "The Last Scotland", along with some of his vendors and his bodyguards. Lito died, I saw him fall , I saw hi bloody chest, and those who would be his next partners died as well. Nothing out of the ordinary, they were traffickers, nothing that went beyond what was expected by the Executor and President Cesare Tovar. Except of course, the young people at the next table, who had just arrived for dinner, or the family chatting by the window. Or the waiters. All of them collateral damage that will not appear in the newspaper report tonight. Impossible to read something that could cloud the perfect mission of the Executor.

The only one who was able to leave the place unscathed was Leggio's bodyguard: **me**.

I've been walking this block since ten at night. It has been three hours since the bloody body of my brother Lito was disposed of in "The Last Scotland", along with other bodies, destroyed by silver bullets from official government silverguns.

But *SyanL* is peace, says Cesare Tovar. *SyanL* is progress and advance, seconded by his Executor.

I've been walking this block since ten in the night and when I finally stop, I won't be the same.

ESTIRGE

"Running over the same old ground, what have we found?

the same old tears.

I wish you were here "

I hurt my hands with the broken marble of some towers that are already damaged by time. I don't care, I walk furiously, stepping on the fucking graves, wanting to sink them deeper and deeper into the fucking earth where our dead are supposed to lie and rest. Fuck that rest. Nobody will ever have a break, not even after dead, nobody with the weight that we, the born in *SyanL* carry, and my father carried me as the heaviest load in his entire life. The golden crosses on the graves shine like lanterns.

I feel the tears wetting my cheeks as I continue walking over the ceilings of high tombstones. It's August, which is even more screwed up. Heat does not combine with mourning. It is unbearable. Finally, I stop when I reach one of the towering cemetery walls. From here, on the borders of *Sy4*, you can see the city in all its beauty. A gorgeous provincial city in the messy country that is *SyanL*. Beautifully constructed buildings, with architectural details so splendid that no one would think that the economic depression of a few years ago hit *Sy4* so hard that it almost died. My beloved city, the brick city, the ocher city that has buildings like this same cemetery, famous throughout the country, it is so famous that people come from other cities to bury their dead, to this Catholic compound, one of the few that remain, golden and sepia in color that generally contrasts with the cobalt blue offered by our cloudy sky. But not today. August and its oppressive heat, august, and its fucking heat.

Suddenly I don't want to look at the city anymore, I want to go back to dad's grave, where just a couple of hours ago he was buried for his "eternal rest", in this soil that he learned so much to hate over the years, or at least that is what he always said. The fucking lies were with us for a long time. Especially those about my mother. Lies that cover a past that I do not want to investigate, lies that I will surely continue to hold all my life, that hurt as much as the fact that dad is gone, that I will no longer smell his cigar breath or his clothes always smelling of *Tino Tawrr*, his favorite whisky or that I will no longer see him leafing through documents, with an eternal desire to have them in scrupulous order.

I want to stop watching the bustle of Sy4, but it is beautiful and I have a nagging weakness for beautiful.

I return in my footsteps; I jump under the roof of the crypt that is next to my father's last home and my mind continues to inquire. My eyes fill with tears again because the old man has already left. As if that were not enough, he has had the cruelty to drop a word bomb before leaving. A pain bomb. I take a handful of sand that glows almost yellow between my fingers and toss it on the headstone, over dad's name.

"You leave me fucked up, alone and fucked up. I don't know what hurts me the most and how can I claim you? Damn! how, if you are gone?" I kick the loose earth on his grave, as if it were really falling on his eyes or in his mouth, as if it really offended the memory of my old father, when surely in heaven or in hell, he must be making fun of me and my tantrums. ***"You have always been a child, you behave like a child, you respond like a child and you think like a child"*** he used to say ***"surely when you love, you will do it like a child and they will fuck you mercilessly"***.

Surely he was saying it because that was how it had happened to him. But no, I was no longer a boy, and I was going to show him.

"And this is, Dad, the only time I visit your grave. The only one" I say, pointing to the tombstone, as if I saw hir small and brown eyes on it "I say goodbye, I will not return again" I finish. But when I turn to walk away, I see a young man dressed in a neat black suit, with a bouquet of flowers in his hand, who looks at me amused. He is probably 18 years old, my own age, if anything a couple of years older. He wears a mustard"colored tie arranged to perfection, I resent the excellence of his image on such a sad day as today.

"Are you coming to fight the dead? Is it some kind of therapy?" He says, placing the flowers in a niche in the elegant crypt that is next to my father's grave.

"Fuck you," I reply and start to walk, ready to walk away. As I pass him I take a quick glance at the inscription in the crypt: *"In memory of my brother, Lito Leggio"* it reads on it.

SILFIDE

"Cause love is such an old fashioned word,

and love dares you to care for the people in the edge of the night "

What in.

I hold the wings of a red butterfly between my thumb and index finger. She is still alive and my fingertips tickle when she tries to move her wings. It has white dots on the icing that frame its pointed wings. Its body is black and shines brightly in the summer sunlight. I like to contemplate them and with time I have learned to catch them, although I always let them fly after a while, it is my hobby. Today is Saturday and I can't handle this boredom, but it's the only day of the week that I can rest, so I go out to the garden and hold butterflies from the wings for several hours. The sun is about to set and I have to go back. Today is the day. I spread my fingers, freeing he, the red body crashing against the yellow sky that illuminates *Sy1* the last minutes of the afternoon. In contrast, the gray mansion waits for me.

"Salvatori Army" reads a laminated sign above the main entrance, the painting on the portico used to be inviting, with a pomegranate tree at the entrance, but today it looks orange and old. It's amazing that in five years they haven't done anything to improve this site. The *"saviors"* complain every day about how difficult it is to get sponsors to feed all

the children, youth and adults who live here and they never forget to mention that they cannot afford to spend their little income on frivolity, such as the façade arrangement or beds or shampoo, or some damn decent blanket for the harsh *SyanL* winters.

Crazy, crazy, crazy, crazy. It's what I think, but I don't tell them, although I was about to do it once, when they wanted to force me to donate my hair so they could sell it.

"Twenty centimeters of red hair would be equivalent to two weeks of tomatoes and watermelon for the children," they had told me, but I did not give in. I overheard their conversation that same night:

"She's just a selfish and vain little girl."

"If it were up to me," Salvadora Viridiana had answered, "I would not only sell her hair, but I would rip out her stupid blue eyes to take away her presumptuousness!"

Today is my last day in this place of *good people,* I am not going to sleep again on a hard mat with scratchy edges, in a room smelling of urine.

I enter the room that I share with other twenty"seven people : seventeen children, four pregnant women, and four elderly people. I go to my corner and put away my precious things (they have no real value, but ... "sentimental"), a dried cherry"colored butterfly, a metal barrette that shines as if it had once been ruby and a sweater that is not as awful as the rest, it has pictures of smiling apples.

With the jeans I'm wearing now, it will be enough to be protected from the cold. I choose the moment, this is it. There is no doubt, everyone is heading to the dining rooms and the Saviors are already there, their personal tables served with the best dishes, while the others will surely have to eat moldy bread and dried fruits. I head for the front door, not that I'm running away, as no one is forcing me to be here. I know that I this hole, you eat regularly, that you have a roof to shelter from the storms that hit SyanL with force in May, but I am not going to stay here, waiting for the day when the Saviors decide to sell my hair and even my eyes in a fit. No, I prefer to suffer the cold, the rain, the sun that dries the skin, the wind that reddens the eyes (at least I will have eyes). I take one last look and say goodbye to what I could never call Family.

When I open the gate and find the bustle of Sy1, the noise of the cars and the indifference of the people of the capital, they make me think that perhaps I should have left the place after dinner.

The dusk decorated with the buildings cheers me up a bit. It is the capital, there must be a thousand ways to survive, I am only nineteen years old and I will find millions of opportunities, they are always looking for young people. Although maybe not on these streets. *Las Salvadoras* refuge is located in the White part of Sy1. They call it like that because of its characteristic situation of being a sector without a clear conquest of authority over it. That is how Salvadora Rocío expressed it and it is evident that she was right.

On the sidewalks there are sales carts, they offer several things: Nexus UP that are practically new, NexNotes even with its packaging and some of the cars sell Whiskey of all prices: Joan Mheggia, Nikolak Leeving, Tinno Tawrr and Jooly Rodz are the most expensive of SyanL , but here they are sold at half price.

It is strange: I am a resident of SyanL, born in the capital and I have only tasted whiskey once in my life. When I turned sixteen, the Saviors celebrated my day with a feast to which I was not invited, same as the other members of the shelter. Around eleven o'clock that night everyone went to sleep and the Salvadoras told me that I could eat some of the bread that was left over from my birthday, as long as I put away the dishes from the table. I remember there was the long, slim reddish glass bottle with just one shot of *Jooly Rodz* one of the finest whiskeys ever. I ate the bread as fast as I could, almost choking on its dryness, for what I was urging was to finally taste what SyanL was prized for on the planet: its whiskey.

I emptied the contents of the bottle into a clean glass and took a sip. The taste had seeped into my throat, making me cough and spit out a few breadcrumbs. I looked around the table, the water bottles were still sealed and the Salvadoras would have killed me if I had dared to open any. In one corner of the table was half a lime juice from one of the ladies, who did not like whiskey because she was from LaGem, not from SyanL.

I filled the glass with the citrus drink and to this day I can assure you that there is nothing that is such an exact combination of strength and sweetness, perfect and ideal.

Now walking through this neighborhood, I wonder how those who buy it here will drink it, those who can only buy whiskey at the hands of a dealer.

Little by little I get away from the bustle of the selling and I get into a small street. The light from the lanterns is weak, some lamps glow yellow and others are completely out. I turn to see how far I have already gotten away from the merchants and it is when I see the figure of a man, a few meters away. It is the first time I have been outside the shelter, yet I can feel that I have never been more in danger than now. I am not rushing my pace and I have no time to think that it is a mistake not to. A hand pulls me and tears the sweater that I have kept safe so much these months. I scream loudly, hoping to get the attention of the merchants but I'm silenced by a forceful blow to the stomach. I can't breathe, I try to look somewhere and I can't, I feel infinite pain in my ribs and I can hear the noise of an engine, my eyes are blocked by tears, the body that was over me is removed and I can see that he runs towards even darker streets. Between the fingers of my right hand I feel a warm hand pressing me and in my left, the torn sweater, I fade away.

DRIDER

<blockquote>

"I am stepping through the door

and I'm floating in the most peculiar way,

and the stars look very different today "

David Bowie.

</blockquote>

I like to visit my friend. I have no friends, Mom and Dad won't let me. My birthday parties do not seem like mine, rather they are my parents' dinners, as when they say: "We have a business dinner, no other children will go, only older parents and gentlemen." There are always more people in black suits at my birthdays than at a funeral. I am already a grown up, I am almost ten years old. They also explain to me as if I were stupid. I'm not, I'm smart, that's why I don't go to school, teachers come to my house, because everyone wants to teach such a smart kid. Yes, I am, I have already understood how some *NexusDesk* programs and one of *Nexus UP* are made, the one that tries to build a cube to form the SyanL map with various colors on a black background. I like programs and technology. Dad says that although SyanL has a good reputation in that, Toot is a much more advanced country in that matter. But I'm not interested in visiting Toot, and even less in living there, Toot is boring.

"There is a new boy at school," Corina tells me as she walks through the library, looking at the dictionaries and translators that her father keeps in the bookshelves.

"What's his name?" I ask her, pretending that I don't care that she does go to school and that she also knows other children. I picture her in her black skirt uniform and blue sweater, with SyanL's crest on a ribbon around her arm.

"I don't know, I didn't pay attention to it," she answers, grabbing a book of mythological stories. I'm relieved to know that she doesn't even remember the name. She also called him "new boy", not friend. I am her friend.

"Do you want to read?" She says. The truth is that I don't want to, but I wouldn't like her to get angry or think that I am stupid and I do not read because I do not attend a school, like her. But she knows that it is not up to me. Mom and Dad would never allow it. I always say that, it is because I am very intelligent, but the truth is different. I don't know which one is the truth, I only know that one day I heard my father tell my grandmother that it was dangerous and that he was not going to risk me, his only son.

I understand Dad, maybe going to school is dangerous, you can fall and scratch, you can vomit if lunch doesn't suit you, you can fight with a child who wants to be friends with Corina, you can catch something or you can pee your pants. Corina told me that this happened to one of her classmates a couple of years ago. So I understand dad.

"Yes" I answer Corina at last "but please, the book of the types of spiders in the world" I ask. She shrugs her shoulders but stands up for the book I asked her, it is an extensive volume that has pictures of spiders, indicating their characteristics, the place where they are found, their poisons and sizes.

I look at her. Corina has a lot of hair, the color of wood. But her laugh is better, she always laughs, and her pretty eyes. I smile when I see her come with the black cover book. I don't know yet that this is the last smile I will have in a long time.

I don't know yet that, that night is the last one I will see Corina until we are both seventeen years old.

I don't know yet that Corina's father is heading to the library with the weight of terrible news that will change my life forever. With a shadow that will haunt me from now on.

I don't know yet that I'm going to live in Toot for a few years, with my grandmother.

I still don't know that half an hour ago my parents were murdered by a group of kidnappers.

I don't know yet that those kidnappers were after me.

I don't know yet that Mom and Dad just sacrificed their lives to protect me.

I don't know yet that I'm about to start hating the world.

21

GORGONA

"And she promises the earth to me and i believe her,

after all this time, i don't know why "

The Beatles

No one has told me anything and I hate them for it. I hate them all, I hope they die. They walk around the living room, through the kitchen, going from here to there, carrying coffee and sugar in the cups of mother's emerald china. I have not moved from this side of the chair, I wait by the phone. My Aunt Tony walks by carrying a tray of cups, offering them with a polite smile. I hate her too. I hate her gesture of having everything under control, her air of being the person in charge of my house right now.

A fleeting feeling of tiredness makes me yawn, I haven't slept in thirty"six hours and that's one of the hardest things. I know I must sleep, try to rest, but I can't. I cannot sink into that, in that other reality that is the dream, only to wake up later and realize that nothing has changed, that the house is still full of government investigators, of class A agents in their military suits and family *solidarity* to me, *poor Corina*. I don't want to sleep to wake up and face the fact that my parents and my brothers are still missing.

I never want to sleep again, but I don't want to stay awake either, I'm sick of this parade of strangers, besides, nothing assures me that it was not one of them who somehow planned the disappearance of my family. It would not be the first time it has happened in SyanL. My parents are active business partners of the whiskey firm *Tino Tawrr.* Dad inherited his part from Grandpa, who rests in peace. He was a majority partner, although he was not always one. My dad was still a child when Grandpa started as the keeper of the barrels and their care. He liked to buy a barrel and have it deducted from his monthly salary. I remember him when he was very old, alone, in the last room of his house, sitting in his dry green chair. Nobody but him sat there. He drank his whiskey in a round, jade"colored glass and played old music. He liked his chair but not rocking chairs, for he used to say that these were for decrepit people. The thought in my head hurts: I want to see my father grow old, and my mother and my brothers. Now I don't know if I will.

I remember my grandfather falling asleep, after drinking his whiskey, in that intimacy of the dream, so lost and loose in that statue state.

I do not want to sleep. I cover my face with my hands, my hair is a tangle of loose hair that more than a day ago had been moistened by the tears that filled my face when I found out. My family has been lost for thirty"six hours, they seem to have disappeared from the face of the earth. I don't know if they are still alive, I don't know the purpose of this, I don't know anything, and the only thing I want is a miracle or to die.

My Aunt Tony sits next to me and checks her Nexus.

"Nothing yet, sweetie," she says, without looking at me, "nothing ..." she sighs. I hate her, I hate her purple lipstick, which contrasts with the lemon she sucks after adding sugar, her gestures are very festive for these moments, I hate her filtring with Inspector Waltz. I hate everything about her, I hate that her face is similar to Mom's, but with green eyes. Mom's are brown and smiling. And yes, I say *are*, in the present tense, because I want them to be alive, because I would give my face, my hands, everything, I would give my life for a miracle to happen and see them enter through that door. Seventeen years are just a few to deal with the loss of my entire family. I still remember the crying, the anger, the hard sadness when I lost my grandfather and I don't want to live it again. I don't know why miracles happen, but I look towards the entrance, fervently wanting one. And it happens.

It confuses me to see him, and I know it's him, even though it's been years. The last time I saw that hair, the last time I saw those big, grey eyes that seem to encompass everything. The last time I saw that cleansing of personality, even though I was just a child back then, when I could only offer my shoulder to cry and then nothing else, not a word, nothing.

I justify myself: I was just a child, like him, I was immature, childish. But guilt, although blurred, has followed me every night: he was my best friend and I was not there when he needed me most.

Today that I thought about dying, for the first time in my life, he appears here.

He looks at me, I know that there is something different and I do not know if it is guilt or if we are joined by a pain that I am afraid to feel, but which is a heavy load that he carries since we were seven years old: the sadness of being alone. The melancholy of the past is reflected in his big gray eyes.

When he approaches me, my first thought is that he would hug me, as all those who now walk around my house with a worried face have done, but it does not happen like that, instead he holds my head with both hands and looks straight at my eyes.

"I am sorry" he says "I'm so sorry, I came in when I found out" he lets go of me, and now we are only two people that know each other, now there seems to be no trace of the intimacy that is shared between friends.

"We don't know anything yet," I explain, without establishing a tone of voice, I don't know how to talk to him and it makes me angry to worry about that, about something like this, at a time when I don't know if my family lives.

"Inspector Waltz told me that they already extended the search to LaGem and Toot, if they don't appear tomorrow, they will continue to La Costa" he explains, for a moment it alarms me that the inspector has been so explicit with him, but how could he not be . Now he, Adolfo Noots, is the sole heir to the fortune and empire of the *Jooly Rodz* bottling company. I know that Adolfo's uncles run the company and that he has lived in the shadows, since he is still scrupulously protected, because after what happened with his family, SyanL cannot afford to lose the nucleus of such an important company. All the partners of the company hope that when he reaches the age of twenty"one, he will take over the bottling plant.

"I understand you and I offer you my full support in whatever you need," he says, taking my hand and squeezing me gently. Aunt Tony watches us with interest as she offers mint tea to some newly arrived relatives. I ignore her curious look.

"Thank you" I answer, I feel ashamed with Adolfo, in all these years I did not lift a finger to look for him, to communicate with him. And his behavior is totally different, since at my first crisis, here he is and I don't know what to say to him. I hug him and hear him mutter:

"Don't worry, everything will change soon, we will change it."

ONDINA

"Maybe I'm learning why the sea on the time has no way of
turning "

Roxy Music.

My mother says that I have a brother named *Diego*. I
don't believe her.

"Diego must be about twenty"two years old by now,
Viviana, unlike you, he always was excited about his birthday,
as it should be" she shares and stares blankly, her eyes fixed
on a past in which she remembers a family member that I
never knew.

I go to the kitchen and heat water in a pink, fine china
mug. It is one of the gifts from her wedding to the man who
replaced my dad, the only one I could save when my mother
got rid of everything that had to do with him. And she did so
with good reason. I sprinkle a powder on it in the water that
instantly turns coral color and I drink it like that. This lonely
atmosphere is sad, something hurts inside me when I feel the
silence that surrounds my mother and me. I go up to my room
carrying the cup of mauve tea and avoid her gaze, which is
still fixed on the family photos of yesteryear. The wall is full
and nowhere does that Diego appear that she talks about so
much.

At times like this I would like to know how to entertain myself in some way. I don't have books, except a love novel and those that refer to school. I have never been the great reader and I have no intention of becoming one. What my life lacks is emotion, not reading. I think about ordering my shoes following some pattern of colors or styles. Shoes I do have enough and sometimes I entertain myself by trying them on, using different types of clothes, but I have done it so many times that I no longer know how to match them.

At seventeen, having a closet full of clothes and shoes must mean some kind of success. My friends share that same hobby and so I don't feel as lonely as when my mother ignores me, thinking of a supposed brother whose existence I do not remember, but who overshadows my place in this house.

"Vivi!" My mother shouts at me, she must have already come out of her lethargic time full of nostalgia. I want to understand her and I want her presence and moments of affection to be enough, but they are not, and it is not her fault. I know how to analyze myself and within myself, I allow myself to be honest: I am not happy.

"Wait a minute!" I say, I put on the fuchsia sweater and check the time, it's six forty, it's time for the daily routine: go to the SyanL Investigation and Loss of People and Property Station. We go every day in order to collect new information from the system. We can only have access from the Nexpads of that building, for security reason.

"We'll be late," she tells me, I don't perceive reproach, but genuine concern.

"Sorry" I reply anyway as an apology. She doesn't answer, I take the car keys and hurry to the door, anticipating her, wanting to establish that I have been on time.

"I wish your father had left some information about Diego, it would make our search easier," she says, once we are in the car, on the way to the Station.

"Yes, I know" I imitate her, but I don't share that opinion. It would have been impossible for Dad to leave any data and that is what bothers me so much: that my mother instead of crying to him, having kept a respectable and dedicated mourning, became obsessed with *Diego* from the first moment.

The building where the Station is located is tall, like the rest of the official departments of this fraction of Sy1. The buildings are white, as in the Health sector, there is no drop of color or life. Very different from the arts sector, or government and especially in the business sector, where the Whiskey companies are located in mahogany and off"white buildings, of a majestic beauty like old Greek theaters, with a modern and technological touch.

I move through the parking lot until I find a free spot. My mother is, as usual, absorbed in her thoughts.

"I hope today is the day," I say trying to sound like her.

"I have hope that it will be," she answers, getting out of the car. I wonder for a moment: if I suddenly disappear, would she look for me with the same eagerness and dedication?

"Viviana, it's already seven o'clock, we have only half an hour to use the equipment and do the search" she hurries me from outside the car.

It is true, as time goes on, we are given less time to search the systems. Six years ago we had three hours, now we only have a half. Mom hugs the folder with the collected information as we go up in the elevator. The list with the record of 552 *Diegos* who would be the age that according to her, my brother should be: twenty"five years old.

We have done some searches at home, but the results of private Nexpads and Nexus are not so reliable, since they create false information that is left on the net, information that it may not be accurate. My mother knows this very well, but she doesn't want to lose hope. As for me, I have lost it myself from a lot of time ago. At first I was excited about the possibility of having a brother, of searching tirelessly with my mother and then, meeting him, like in the movies, but not anymore. I'm starting to get fed up of looking at myself from the outside and observe the depression that has filled my house for years. And not for my father, as it should be, but for someone that I am not sure exists. We will never find him, in case his life is real, I know that she will never see him again and that I will never know him. SyanL, in addition to being famous for whiskey, is also famous for being one of the countries with the highest reported disappearances, mostly due to crime. But *Diego* may have fled, may have taken on a different personality or may already be dead.

We enter the search room, it is full of people who come to the same thing that us. I look for a place, we walk between cubicles, in some there are up to five people crowded together, nothing strange to see a whole family looking for someone. In others there is only one person and it is sadder. Mom and I finally found *03087N* free. She rushes to turn on the Nexpad which immediately responds, giving a mechanical welcome:

"WELCOME, CITIZEN, TO ACCESS THE SYSTEM, ENTER YOUR PASSWORD" indicates the hollow voice of the recording. Mom follows the instruction and types four numbers and two letters.

"WELCOME CARMEN METZOL, REMEMBER THAT WHEN YOU ARE USING THE SYANL SEARCH SYSTEM, THE ACCESS TO HAVE YOUR DATA AND SEARCHES WILL BE STORED FOR PURPOSES OF IMPROVEMENT IN THE SERVICE" continues the voice, mom gets impatient and with her finger presses the lower edge of the screen, accessing the protocol, the voice pauses "THANKS" it finally says, offering us the SY4000 search engine on the screen. Mom starts looking and I mark the name of the next Diego on the list with a bright pink marker.

"In the name of the Blessed Sacrament," my mother murmurs, rescuing the Catholicism that she only remembers when she is looking for Diego. When I see her, I feel a terrible desire to cry, to scream, to get out of there, to abandon everything. But I can't imagine how I could, nor do I see myself daring to abandon her. The screen shows information about this new Diego, but the date of birth does not match.

"It could be an error, it is common that sometimes the records in the network have the wrong number" she says and chooses the Search in Detail option. I nod, even though she doesn't see me. Voices in the next cubicle catch my attention, I try to listen.

"It's not going to work" is the voice of a girl, I turn around discreetly, I am good at that. I see her and her very presence amazes me, she has long brown hair, and her eyes, even from this distance, look intense and concerned.

"Fool is the one who doesn't try," says a guy next to her, he has defined features and straight hair that gets in the way of his eyes, which look smaller when he smiles. His brown look makes me nervous, even when he is not looking at me.

"I don't know, I'm scared to find something that could hurt me."

"That is so you" says the other one who is with her, he has tanned skin and big gray eyes "since you were a child, you are like this" he continues, who unlike them, dresses elegantly, wears a black suit and a red tie , with a small hourglass designed in the knot of it.

"It is rather a characteristic in almost all the people from Sy4, my father was like that, and I think I am also a bit like that, although not in such an extreme way as you, Corina" clarifies the one with straight hair, who wears jeans and a honey color sweatshirt, which despite its simplicity suits him well.

"I don't understand what makes you think I'll find something here. The SyanL search team leaders themselves are conducting an investigation" she says nervously. Her hair is down, a few strands brush her nose and cheeks, but she doesn't seem to mind. I don't know what prompts me to undo my braid at that moment, so that my hair looks similar to hers. I am not sure it would look the same,, since hers looks shiny and I hope mine does too.

"Let's go" she asks, I hope the other two don't listen to her, I don't want them to leave, for some reason I need to keep listening to them.

"Make a single try" says the one with straight hair "please."

"I'm scared, Jimmy" she looks at him "I have gotten used to the idea that they are still alive and that one day they will return, without searching, without making any effort" she says, they? Who is he referring to? Friends? Family? She looks too young to have children. Maybe he refers to her brothers. It makes me smile that she may be in the same situation as me. I don't know why, but I would like that. I feel the gaze of the guy with straight hair and jeans on me, he has realized that I was listening to them. He observes me as analyzing me and I feel that I have never experienced something like this in my life, at this moment, when I wear my hair down like her, and deep brown eyes are on me.

CHAPTER

1

I have two rules than are more important than any well"assembled procedure in Drider's head: Be discreet, be quick.

People walk and I feel their energy, it is contagious and that motivates me, I look up and the intense gray of the sky hits me in the eyes. My long hair, usually unruly, now sits in a low ponytail, just like the one in the girl in front of me or the one walking behind me, or anyone else. They all wear black, just like me, I think that there are close to 40,000 people, all chanting the same cry demanding justice for Sy1 and Sy3. I slow my step and slowly move to the right, then I see it: the green door that Estirge showed me on the map a month ago is barely visible and if he hadn't shown me, I'm not sure I could have located it now. I continue to slide slowly when I hear her voice in the tiny earpiece, which I have stuck in my ear, it is the size of a mole, barely perceptible.

"Gorgona, do you see the door?" He says, I clear my throat once, so that the small microphone on my neck, another mole, transmits the information "perfect" he continues "it's clear, I'll see you on the roof in three minutes" he finishes and I have to admit, his help is very useful.

I slide through the door while outside people continue to advance, I still feel the intention of their fury on my skin and with it, a certain satisfaction for what I am about to do. Estirge was right, the building is empty, but before climbing the stairs, I look carefully: there are no sensors in sight and the circular sights with SyanL colors, blue and gold, have been deactivated. I don't know if that was the work of Estirge or Drider, but it doesn't matter.

I pull on the hood of my coat and stick to the wall I climb up the stairs, my right hand in my pocket, just in case.

Outside the protest continues and despite the fact that it was announced months ago, the Executor of Justice and Command insisted on giving his annual speech. People hate him from the deepest splinter of their bones, especially those who have been punished by SyanL and although the President is the one in the forefront, when it comes to carrying out The Night of Punishments, is the Executor whom we see in SyVisión, it is his face in charge of reading the names of the punished, before their execution or on less serious occasions, the confiscation of their property. A noise makes me stop, I feel that usual lump in my throat, but it is only the wind that moves some broken glass. *Nothing happens*, I tell myself. I see the door that leads to the roof and still attached to the wall I get to it.

"Estirge?" I whisper before opening the door.

"*Vorwärts*" he answers, in German. Each of us has an ancient language assigned for that one indication: *go ahead*. His is German. I open the door and see him chest"earth near the edge, covering himself with some old and rickety iron, his hair blowing in the wind.

"You must wear the cap of your hoodie, your hair can be seen from a thousand kilometers" I say, approaching, and it is true, his hair reaches his ears and it moves a lot. I imitate his chest"to"ground position as I go next to him.

"Focus Gorgona, you can't fail in this one, it's 200 thousand for you and 100 thousand for me"

He says no more, the people twenty floors below continue to advance in their movement, showing an intense rage. I manage to read some signs JUSTICE WITHOUT BLOOD!, A WHISKEY IS WORTH MORE THAN MY LIFE, MY BROTHER DIED FOR A STOLEN BOTTLE, THE NATION IS A KILLER!, SYANL: CORRUPTION AND CRUELTY!, WE WANT EACH OTHER ALIVE… All are right, except the first, justice almost always requires blood.

I see it, I see the complete scene, the Executor Maurice Mon De Plaza has taken the stand, he is with more government people, they all are dressed with elegance and neatness…*don't look at them for long,   just record the environment in the head,* those are the words of Estirge that I never obey.

With the care in which a baby is carried, I take the golden weapon, a goldgun900 from my right pocket, the contact with my skin has made it warm. I aim and squint, the bright color of the weapon fusing in my vision with the Executor's face. When I shoot no noise is heard, but in a matter of seconds, Maurice Mon de Plaza falls to the ground. It will take five minutes for the wound to show up on his forehead, because I know what I'm doing. This is the exact amount of time that we have to get on Estirge's motorcycle, and get away from here.

CHAPTER

2

We will travel to the coast in a couple of hours. The plane leaves at five forty-five. I've been drinking the same cup of coffee since Estirge dropped me off at my apartment a while ago. I have packed everything I need in a white suitcase with bright flowers, very springy, except for the tiny golden snake on the edge, just like the one I have hung around my neck since I was sixteen, small, shiny and gold with some details green.

Forty-eight months using my alias and I have grown fond of its symbol. We have all done it with our own, in our own way. Dulce, for example whose nickname is Silfide, the wind fairy, seductive and capricious, she tattooed some red wings on her abdomen, around her navel and when she did, she showed them to us with pride:

"In case you ever have to identify my body, this is the seal of authenticity."

"I would need to touch the seal of authenticity," Satiro had answered with his half-smile grin, "to be sure." Silfide's answer was a decisive middle finger.

"Then don't show, if you're not willing to play" he replied, loosening his tie, a gesture he makes constantly when he complains about something.

"Satyr, you get *excited* even with your pillow."

"My pillow always looks like it wants something," he had told her. Jair's alias is Satiro and underneath his wavy brown hair, although he wears it short, he has a horn outlined with the razor. It is unable to see, unless we lift his hair, which is impossible without him taking it as flirting. No one would think that this attractive and elegant young man of twenty, who owns suits, tuxedos, and tailcoats of all kinds and models, has a shaved symbol on his head. Although in the same way, no one would think that he is a cold-blooded murderer.

Adolfo... my childhood best friend... he refuses to mark his skin, his hair or to wear hangings. His nickname, *Drider*, is reflected in the collection of spiders that he has in his bedroom desk.

"You need a symbol in you and nobody wants you to go through life carrying one of your little friends" I had told him, referring to his spiders, three years ago when we decided on symbols and aliases.

"I could train one of them..."

"Drider, do it and you'll have to do the job alone," Silfide had complained.

"I always do it alone," he used to say slyly.

"Please, a symbol," I insisted. The next day, no one said anything when the small red hourglass that characterizes the black widow was marked on his wristwatch.

It's cold and I like it, but it doesn't matter, since after every job we all leave our little country, at least until the matter is forgotten. The money was in my account and in Estirge's account fifteen minutes after the death of the executor was announced globally, on each Nexus.

Jimmy ...He has a small, clear mole on his right cheek, almost next to his lip, it is shaped like a drop. He painted it red himself, so if you look closely at his face and if he's not smiling, it looks like a drop of blood. It's tiny, but for me, it's very present.

"Your alias is very vampiric for my liking" Satiro had told him, and he had a reason: the mythological *Estirge* sucks the blood of its victim to death and that at the same time, gives it life.

"It reminds me more of a mosquito," was Drider's opinion.

"Look who's talking: the faun of Narnia and Spiderman."

It is very easy to upset him and they know it, the three of them are so violent that it surprises me how the six of us are still alive.

My Nexus rings, a tone very familiar to me, it's Ondina.

"We are at the airport, only you are missing, Gorgona."

"I'm on my way," I say and hang up. Before leaving I quickly check myself: brown curls, makeup, pink coat, and high-heeled boots. I am nothing like the *me* of a few hours ago. But today we are young heirs, looking for vacations and parties on the beaches of La Costa, it is a very safe disguise. I really look different, except for the snake on my neck. *Gorgona*, like medusa, that's the reason of my symbol, nobody ever calls me *Corina* so far.

Viviana's is a mermaid since her alias is *Ondina*. She also wears a hanging, very similar to mine, but in the shape of a mermaid.

"Original," Silfide had said mockingly, Ondina's reaction had been to lower her gaze, with some discomfort. I don't blame her, nobody likes to be reminded of her tendency to imitate others.

"They are not the same" I had said "hers is silver and mine is gold"

"What a big difference!"

"Enough" I shut her up suddenly. It was necessary, poor Ondina, sometimes it was difficult for her to get along with Silfide, but who it is normal I think. When I met her she also intimidated me a bit.

I love them both and I would give my life for them both, without hesitation, without asking.

One hour to board. Upon my arrival I see them waiting and they don't seem like the group of killers that they really are. The confident and seductive face of Satiro, the beauty of Silfide, they seem taken from fiction. Drider listens to music, relaxed, checking his Nexus. Ondina talks to Estirge, he drinks coffee and she smiles at him. I don't like it, I feel a pressure in my chest that I only regularly experience when I pick up a gun.

"Ready?" I ask, approaching. Ondina nods with a smile, I try to return the gesture, but it doesn't come to me.

"Always late," Estirge tells me, checking the time on his Nexus.

"Always exaggerating, you guys haven't even handed over the boarding pass, I know you obsess over everything, but now why with punctuality?" I ask and he shrugs. This always happens, I imagine how we see ourselves from the outside and I know that we can all notice a certain perversity, in our eyes, in our gestures, in our voice, our movements. Everyone except him and that's what he's worth.

"Shall we get on?" Asks Silfide, stifling a yawn.

"Eh… yes" I answer distractedly, then I notice that she is not talking to me, but to Satiro, who, being barely 4:50 in the morning, is already wearing an elegant beige suit, in perfect condition.

As we go to the corresponding room, I see the news of the Executor on each screen of the airport. There are no responsible yet. It's a matter of time before they catch any minor enemies he's had and expose him as a scapegoat. *So SyanL.*

"No" Estirge whispers to me when he catches me watching the screen "remember that you must not… " a lady of a certain age looks at us, I don't have time to feel nervous at the question in her eyes, because Estirge hugs me and kisses me on the cheek so softly that it barely feels and it disappoints me.

"You know very well the two reasons why you shouldn't be watching the news" he says and kisses my face again, with the intention of hiding, this time I do feel the corners of his lips "you put yourself in evidence and you feel guilty" I understand what he is referring to but his words seem to have double meaning in my head. He's right, I know, and I also know that his gesture doesn't mean anything, that it's pure montage to be able to tell me things without raising suspicions from strangers. We do it all the time, everyone. A couple of years ago, Satiro kissed me on the lips for several minutes, to lose sight of a mobile reviewer. But when Estirge gets closer, it's different. I watch him as he hands over his pass and heads to the next level of the airport. He does not wear a suit, he wears jeans and a white shirt, dark glasses and tennis shoes. Drider passes after him,

"Do you have to take your books everywhere?" He says, annoyed by Estirge's huge hand luggage "Do you plan to read them all on the plane? The coast is an hour and a half away? You know it, don't you?"

I lose sight of them when they go to the next level. I still feel the warmth on my face, where he kissed me. I hand over my boarding pass and don't even thank the attendant as I pass by.

And then… **hell**: It's as if the floor was suddenly pulled from me, when I see my killer colleagues against the wall, their hands held in thick, gold handcuffs. Nearly 40 level A guards pointing finer weapons at them. As they handcuff me, I hear the inevitable and feel like vomiting.

"Corina AT, citizen of the SyanL Nation, born in the city of Sy4, on behalf of the President of the State, Mr. Daniel Delonge Chevalier and through the Level A Militia, with delegation 27, you are under arrest for the crime of homicide of the former Executor Maurice Mon De Plaza, with identification plate 3001MN of the Nation of SyanL.

CHAPTER

3

I tremble. My throat is dry and the bones of my wrist tremble against the coldness of the handcuffs that imprison me. In front of me are three level B guards and three of level A. Next to me are two other level A guards. I feel that little by little I will be unable to pass saliva. We're in different vehicles, I haven't been able to talk to them, I haven't even been able to give them a damn look. I examine the truck where they transport me. It is sealed, as if they are transporting wealth and do not want anyone to interfere. My ankles are also held by even thicker handcuffs. None of the eight guards points at me, they know it would be more risky to put weapons within reach. I wish I hadn't chosen this dress so short. And I wish I wasn't such an idiot to worry about a dress when I've been arrested. Arrested. Four years playing very well, to the point of perfection this fucking game! ... And now.

They will kill us, or lock us up for life, no question. The six of us, we have killed nearly eighty people, from corrupt and cruel civil servants to murderous and perverse businessmen. We don't kill good people, ever. But we charge dearly for killing the bad guys. And we don't regret doing it, although this may be a good time to start regretting it.

"There are no good or bad people," silfide had said once, "a human being can be both, depending on the harm or good they do to you."

Nineteen years, I still have too many to live locked in a compact cell. Or maybe they'll kill me, maybe they'll just disappear us, it wouldn't be the first time that happens in SyanL. Or perhaps the State will dress in glory shouting our capture and exposing us to the people as the murderers of the most important political and economic leaders.

We have been traveling for about an hour. This shit does not have a window to know where we are going, to know if they take us to the same place, to see my friends before they die, to search Estirge's face with an answer, although I have no idea which one is the fucking question.

Will President Delonge dare to kill us? His face, his expression in photographs, posters, television, is not that of a bully, rather he is a thin man, blue eyes overshadowed by thin glasses, with the appearance of a university professor, his defined cheeks perhaps too youthful, give him an inexperienced appearance, like one who lives in fear of everything: of the riots in Sy1 and Sy3, of the betrayal in his cabinet, because betraying in SyanL is the daily bread, and above all... he may be scared of the increasingly great threat to SyanL, represented by the president of Toot, the neighboring country.

Both nations are the main exporters of Whiskey throughout the world, and little by little, the quality of Toot's products is growing and there is no other reason than the active and fierce economy of that country, a situation that began about 19 years ago. But that is not the only thing that keeps them growing economically in a field that is ours: there are extensive reports on the hand of Lola Teheran, president of Toot, in the corruption that exists within SyanL, dirty money and adulteration of the whiskey that is produced in SyanL. Probably those are the issues that should keep president Delonge busy, not the capture of a group of young people like us.

They have taken my Nexus, my luggage, my cards, and passport. They checked my retina and took my blood with a very fine tube, which they later closed, sealed and numbered. My blood is A Plus, not very common; if they ever need a transfusion, my blood type would give me priority in search engines for its rarity. However also as a citizen of SyanL, I have an obligation to donate, especially if the emergency comes from a private hospital. One occasion I donated for Bea Morquecho, General Secretary of the SyanL Air Militia, who was in the ER care due to an "accident" or at least that was the official version. That same blood I donated to her trickled onto her bed when six months later, Drider buried a thin, silver dagger in Bea's heart. My partner received 350 thousand bills for that atrocity.

I wonder if any of my friends have already devised a plan or if they have already escaped, I also wonder if they are already dead. I feel so surrounded that I even imagine that the guards can guess what I am thinking. I look down because my fear is so ridiculous that I'm sure they know it, they know what I think, they must be studying my eyes, my lips, my skin. Inside my head, one by one, the deaths that I have carried out for four years are parading. The Director of Television Communication, the heir to the Empire of NexusPhonia, the famous group of the "4 beetles", whose position as bankers had defrauded large SyanL whiskey companies, then moved to Toot and handed over millions of earnings to President Lola Tehran .

Ondina and I took care of the four, but none of them had a violent death; we inject them with the Deli virus. Silfide traveled to the foreign nation of Mahat to bring the content in a fountain pen. 5 milliliters were enough for each of the beetles. The Delí virus is one of the most terrifying biological disasters in the East; a quarter of the population of the distant Mahat has died from it. It is named after Delilah, the biblical character from ancient Catholicism. The infected person loses strength almost instantly and the fever strikes him in a few minutes, stopping his heart. Two beetles drank it, one in cognac, since they didn't used to drink whiskey, the other in a harmless morning mimosa.

Ondina was more risky, she infected the third in a bar with a toothpick that he put in his mouth, but thanks to that audacity, the cause of his death was registered as an accident, since when he left the bar, he drove his car with no chance of survival on the desertic roads of SyanL.

I don't know how my partner executed the fourth, but when the body was found next to that of Mika Lakita, the underwear model, they were both infected with the virus, as if it had spread through their nervous system for several hours.

I am getting used to the movement of the vehicle when it stops. None of the guards say anything, but they put dark glasses on me, they are not sun glasses, they are special and they hug gently over my eyes, I can't see anything, there is no light that comes through them, everything is dark space. For the first time in a long time, I am scared, and I would like to hold a hand between mine, that could give me the courage, even a little of it. I squeeze my eyes tightly, my stomach is queasy, I wish to pass out and not be here.

Two pairs of hands pull me to stand on my feet and I feel the urge to cry or scream, but my dry throat won't do it. The warmth of a close body and after a punch to the stomach that collapses me, the tears come suddenly and an even stronger hit fuels my desire to return. I can hear laughter in the distance and then nothing.

CHAPTER

4

Everything is still black, my first thought when I wake up is that it is night, then the second is that I have gone blind and startled, I try to sit up, but my stomach hurts and my arms are handcuffed to this bed, wrists and of the forearms. I am not blind, my face tense and attached, it indicates that I am still wearing my glasses.

At some distance from where I am, someone complains, it's just a slight sound, but I notice even that in him.

"Estirge?" I whisper, talking causes me pain, my lips feel cracked and dry, my voice seems dusted with sand, I try to swallow to produce saliva, but I can't, everything is pain.

"Gorgona? Are you okay?" His voice is not very different from mine, he seems to have a bad cold, as if he had spent the night screaming and I don't know if he is whispering as a precaution or because he cannot speak louder.

"Yes" I say "it hurts everything on me, even what I don't have, but yes I guess I'm ok, and you? What happened?"

"They caught us" Silfide's voice surprises me, it is heard much clearer and more vigorous than ours "to the six of us"

"Are you okay?" I ask, with each word I hurt my lips more with the effort.

"Yes, and you too, from what I see, from what I have seen in the last hours" she explains "I am not wearing those ridiculous glasses that you have, but I am tied to the bed, I woke up a couple of hours ago."

"Where are we?" I insist "describe the place" I ask my friend.

"There's not much to describe" she sighs "it's a white hospital room, next to the wall is Estirge's bed, then you and me at the end. You have a little blood on your lips" she says and I feel uncomfortable for some reason "and..." she stops, I fear the worst, someone entered, or she fainted, or Estirge has no legs or something similar!

"What?" Estirge insists nervously.

"And my arms are full of bruises, they look horrible" she confesses and I want to kill her, they almost destroyed my ribs and she worries about a few bruises.

"What else?" He asks.

"There are no screens, no fixed communicators, but on the ceiling there is a mobile camera, the size of my head" she explains.

"Microphones?" I ask.

"Two, one on the wall, next to Estirge and one next to my bed," she indicates. Every word we have said will reach the ears of whoever has us here, who has done this to us. I no longer want to talk, I don't even understand why we are using nicknames, our belongings have been taken from us and surely they already know who we are and other information.

"The three of us," continues Silfide, "are wearing a horrible green robe, it seems to be made of ordinary plastic, it doesn't look good, it's very ..." Her voice stops, the sound of a door opening fills me with terror.

"What do you want?! Who are you?!"

"What is it?, Silfide, *who* is it ?, What is happening??"

"NO! What are you doing? NO!"

I try to think with all the clarity that my friend's screams allow me, they don't do anything on me, whatever it is, they are doing it to Estirge.

"No!" I shout suddenly "NO!"

My cries and pleas are confused with those of my partner and then I feel a slight sting in my arm. I do not realize, the darkness before my eyes continues and I sleep.

CHAPTER

5

The feeling that comes to me as soon as I open my eyes is the same headache that I feel when I stay up late. The room is white, as Silfide had well described, the sunlight does not penetrate because the curtains are tightly closed and the dim lamp is enough to cause this almost instantaneous headache.

The beds next to me are empty, but I barely cover my eyelids with my index finger and thumb to dim the light, the door opens and as instinctively I put my fists on guard, that's when I notice that my wrists and forearms are not tied to bed anymore.

"At last! We saw you through the screen" says Drider, taking my hand, I don't let him take it , I still feel nervous and I distrust. He makes a gesture of pain that has nothing to do with the one I feel, but he erases his gesture in a moment, he avoids looking vulnerable, he has always hated to be taken like that.

The five are dressed in white, they look like nurses. Silfide has tied her blouse around her body, the rest don't seem to be in the mood to look good.

"How do you feel?" Estirge asks me and I don't like that either; They treat me like the sick woman, like the poor thing who suffered when they themselves don't look much better than me. However, they are on their feet, they woke up earlier. I feel like I'm walking away and seeing them through a nexusCam. It is then that the big question arises and I drop it without further ado:

"Where are we?" I say, they look at each other. Ondina searches Estirge's eyes nervously. I hate them, I hate them for leaving me out of whatever it is that they know and I don't. Satiro puts a hand on my thigh and winks at me.

"Everything is fine, sweetheart" he murmurs, I look at his hand on my leg, how the hell does he have the peace of mind to caress me at this moment? I hate them!

"It's enough Jair, leave her alone" Estirge also directs his gaze towards Satiro's hand touching me. He called him *Jair*, he didn't use his alias.

"I demand that you tell me what the hell is going on here! Who did this to us?" I feel ridiculous because I am still bedridden, and they are standing.

"They will explain it to you soon" Ondina answers, her tone of sympathy annoys me, she talks to me like my aunt Tony spoke to me many years ago, telling me that my family had disappeared. I ignore her and take a deep breath.

"So?" I ask, impatient "Have they already explained it to you? Why the hell don't you tell me? Aren't we a damn team? Or am I no longer part of it?" I insist, every time raising the voice more; the only one staring at me is Drider, I look at his hands to avoid meeting his gaze, I can see that he has been biting his nails.

"We could say something ... " he begins, looking at Satiro, who does not flinch, calmly refuses, while his finger continues, now on my knee.

"Drider, there are microphones everywhere and we are not authorized to explain anything to Gorgona" Silfide reminds him "also, the truth is that we do not know clearly, they have told us what is strictly necessary, so we are in the same bag" she ends, now she doesn't look harmed, I remember that she had told us that she had some bruises on her arms, but from what I see these have been disappearing. How long have I been asleep? How much advantage information will they have over me?

It smells of alcohol and soap, the pit of my stomach fills with sudden disgust. I don't know if it is due to the fact that my most intimate friends in recent years know something that I do not, but there is discomfort in the environment, it shows when they avoid looking into each other's eyes. I take my time and examine them. Ondina's hair is dull and she wears something on her index finger, maybe It has been broken, she has a scar on the side of her face that she tries to hide with her hair and some pimples on her cheeks out of dryness. Satiro has small wounds on his cheeks, they look like deep scratches, but other than that, he doesn't seem to have been seriously injured. Drider has scars from cuts on his neck, almost on his chest, but they are not the result of high"risk injuries, he has another scar on his mouth, as if he had been bitten.

As for me, I no longer feel any pain, but I can't stand it that they don't inform me, don't even try to.

"Stop touching my leg" I look at Satiro, I try to express my annoyance in some way.

"You seemed to like it," he replies with his lopsided smile, as if this were the most normal thing, as if instead of being murderers locked in something that looks like a madhouse, we were a couple of college graduates celebrating in a bar.

"No one gave me any massage" Silfide complains "I am very offended with you guys" she looks at the three of them, the only one who responds smiling is Satiro.

"That thing is not a massage" Estirge says, his voice is clear again, they laugh and even if I wanted to, I don't. The only thing I want to know now is what's going on.

And I'm about to find out.

The door opens: a woman with stunning green eyes, like the bottom of a bottle, enters accompanied by an escort of level A guards. I recognize her instantly, she is Reneé Lobo, the new Executor.

RENEÉ LOBO

"I need an easy friend, I do with an ear to lend "

Kurt Cobain.

"What about ...?" Daniel looks at the cream"colored paper in the folder that I just handed him a few minutes ago. He marks a name with the silver pen in his hand "Jair Abella Tatchert?" He looks at me through the very thin glass of his glasses. I smile unintentionally when I see him interested in my opinion, although this does not represent anything new, he has always done it. He trusts very much in my thinking.

"There is no *leader* in the *Animalium*" I raise my eyebrow with a dismissive gesture. This bunch of spoiled kids aren't going to truncate my relationship with Daniel "but if there were, he's who could be, if forced. His qualities and specialties are greater than those of the rest" I summarize "his alias is *Satiro*" I indicate, Daniel laughs as if telling himself an inside joke.

"Who chooses these nicknames?" He asks, almost amused.

"They themselves" I say, I don't find it funny, but apparently he does.

"Ingenious children" he observes and underlines another name.

"Jimmy Atkint T., *Estirge*?" Daniel looks at me again, something vibrates in my skin every time I feel like he requires my help "is he second in command?

"No. As I mentioned, there is no leader, therefore there is no replacement for him. They are all the same and they all have a large number of prominent victims to their credit" I suggest carefully and pass on the file of names. All of them represent a very tainted situation in various sectors of the government that Daniel presides over. He thinks for a moment and takes off his glasses, bites the temple of his glasses. The sound of his voice, the freshness in it, like the one of a radio journalist from many years ago makes me think profoundly.

"If these kids, Reneé, are as effective and voracious as this paper indicates to me, then there are two situations that we urgently need to repair" he looks at me and as much as I pride myself on my intelligence, my mind works at a thousand kilometers per hour, but my brain doesn't seem to find what would be ideal to suggest to my President. I don't answer, I blush and curse inside. Daniel puts the paper on the desk and continues:

"The first and most urgent: How the hell is it possible that our Security system is so old and weak as to allow us to lose so many people from the Government? so many pillars of the System?" His voice is not so high, but it is enough to make me feel bad, even though I had barely been in the position of Executor for two weeks "what the hell did that asshole Javier Mon De Plaza do during all his management? that fucking mediocre man!" He exclaims, before putting his index finger and thumb on the bridge of his nose, seeking calm. He closes his eyes for a couple of seconds and continue "it is urgent to correct the many errors or we risk running the same fate ourselves"

"Don't worry about it," I tell him, and I mean it. Nothing matters to me as much as SyanL. Nobody matters to me as much as Daniel Delonge. He and I, together, are going to clean and drain the rot on which our country, our system, is built.

"And the second and most important" he continues, his blue and crystalline eyes, almost transparent, return to show themselves within a stillness that only the President of a nation in chaos can show "you have been in office for two weeks, two weeks and still you have not been able to put these mortuary kids at our disposal… what the hell have you been doing then, Reneé? Playing house and lovers?" he says. I bite my lip furiously. Yesterday he was the one who asked me to move in together.

CHAPTER

6

SyanL is a big country, shaped like a smile, the capital Sy1 is located where a fang would be. Flying over it is something that for the six of us has become routine, but not today. Today we traveled in a steel-colored jet, so bright it bothered my eyes as soon as I saw it. It has ten seats arranged in pairs; I share the place with Estirge, who nervous, does not take his eyes off Reneé. She partly owes us her new position, you might say. I look at her discreetly, she has short blonde hair, her eyes are the central and important point of her face, it is evident that as a child she must have been very pretty and surely a beautiful teenager. Now she is 44 years old, according to the report we read days ago, when we planned the death of the former executor, however, her nose and cheeks are battered by the natural wrinkles that every woman has, but that are accentuated in her. I do not know if the position she occupies and being face to face with the murderers of the former holder of her position make her look older. I meet her palm-colored eyes and quickly turn my gaze to the window of the plane. I don't like this, they haven't told us anything, although at least I no longer feel left out.

When Reneé informed on entering my room that we would have to accompany her immediately and without asking questions, everyone put on the same confused face.

"How do you feel?" Estirge asks me, he likes to put that paternal tone of care and concern.

"I'm ok, thank you" I reply, his brown eyes look at me as if expecting me to ask the same thing, but I still don't want to.

I look at the others, far from looking like prisoners, with these elegant black suits that they have given us, we look like a complete team of lawyers. The only one who looks the same as always is Satiro since this is his usual wardrobe.

"Do you want me to bring you a bottle of water?" Asks Estirge, pretending to get up from his place, as if waiting for my indication "they must have pills, in case your head hurts, or if we ask them, perhaps"

"No thanks, I don't want anything" my voice may have raised more than normal, because everyone on the plane turns to see us, one of Reneé's guards even raises a gun.

Again I focus on the window, wishing I knew what could have gone wrong in the plan, where did we fail? How did they catch us?

"I understand your attitude" insists my partner, I can not avoid a gesture of annoyance, narrowing my eyes, which does not seem to matter to him "but you must also understand that we really did not know anything, only that Reneé had gone to see us when each one we woke up, but she didn't say anything to us" I feel the warmth of his fingers when his hand is placed on mine "we are all nervous" he ends and as if everything was programmed, at that moment, Reneé stands up.

"We will land in Sy4 in minutes, I suggest you do not try little games of any kind, because when you go down there will be about a hundred level A guards to receive us, save yourself the trouble of trying to flee and die trying."

"May I ask-" Silfide begins.

"No, you may not" Reneé interrupts. It is evident and even if we could, she will not tell us a thing. My friend looks at her with hatred, but Reneé seems to enjoy playing with us like that. Satiro turns to see Silfide and moved his head no, I manage to see that his lips murmur "idiot", but his gesture is still mocking.

"We're about to land," the Executor informs, returning to her seat.

Looking out the window, I know it's Sy4, but I don't understand, we're not heading to the airport, we're heading to a runway surrounded by pine trees and an imposing building on one side, with a brick facade, like almost everything in Sy4. I don't know why, but I must keep this image in my head.

CHAPTER

7

I barely set foot on the ground, four level A guards handcuff and hold me. I have no weapons, no strength, or any idea that motivates me to want to escape, but even so, whoever is behind this, considers that I and the others need to be guarded by fifteen guards each.

As we walk to the golden brick and glass building, a cool breeze plays with my hair, it's the first pleasant sensation in days. Well, no. It is the second, the first occurred on the plane, a few minutes ago, with his hands. But I don't have time to think about it as we stop in front of the building.

To enter, Reneé types something on the screen of the door and it opens. Upon entering, the number of guards is reduced and now there are only five for each of us. It must be a maximum-security site if they have the confidence to reduce our custodians. For a moment I think maybe it is a prison, but if from the outside the place did not look like a prison, inside the idea of this being a jail, is equal to zero.

The luxury of this place is impressive, it doesn't compare to any of the hotels we have been in, although it looks like one of them. This first floor is very similar to a lobby, there are black leather armchairs and screens on the walls, the floor is so much like a mirror that it is incredible that it doesn't shatter under our feet. Details in gold bricks and blue glass dress the walls.

"This way" says Reneé, we follow her towards an elevator where surely we will not fit with all our entourage of guards who by the way, stick excessively to the body, especially that Silfide's and according to the status of the militia, it is a requirement basic to maintain chastity and give yourself to the SyanL Nation in its entirety.

"From here, I will take charge" announces Reneé when the elevator opens, "go ahead." She orders.

Ondina looks at me with fear as I enter, I smile to give her confidence, but I don't know if this elevator will actually lead us to some kind of punishment or an execution itself. Reneé presses button 13 on the elevator.

"Funny" comments Sátiro, looking at her "I thought that in general buildings the 13th floor is never mentioned or taken in account" he smiles at her. Oh, please, I hope he is not trying to seduce her, I will feel embarrassed when she sends him to hell. She is the Executor and she is not going to play such an obvious game.

"I find your point of view on grace very interesting, Jair, your sense of humor must be quite simple, if a number in a flat seems funny to you" she says, calling him with authority by his real name.

I knew it. Satiro narrows his eyes, offended, you could say that his physical attractiveness and his sense of humor are his best loves and they have just reduced both to ridicule, but what did he expect?

The elevator stops, I can feel Ondina trembling behind me. We are all afraid, we all want to know how to escape, Drider is the only one who seems to look calm. He once told us, a few months ago, that if one day on a mission, he was killed, he would accept without any question, because when it comes to life's wishes, he had never been left wanting anything. Then he said that there is actually an ambition that he has not fulfilled, but he did not come to confess to us what it was about. Now he may no longer have a chance to fulfill it.

Reneé leads us through a corridor that has the same finesse as the rest of the building, a bone color that shines, it seems that it is the very peak of luxury. But it's not like that, we haven't seen anything yet.

She types another password in one of the doors at the end of the hall, she ushers us in. There are six individual chairs in front of a huge white screen, as if it were an old private cinema.

There is also a black desk with a blue glass NexPad.

"Go ahead and have a seat," she says. From her Nexus she deactivates the handcuffs that fall gently from our hands.

"Sit down and enjoy the little show, he'll be with you in a moment."

He?

She leaves us with even more doubts than before.

"What the hell?" Says Estirge, but we don't have time to answer. The screen turns on and a three-dimensional image of Ondina is projected.

"Is it me?" hesitates my friend.

"We'd better sit down" suggests Drider, we obey him without taking our eyes off the image of Ondina on the projection.

It also shows a series of information that although we know it, we are surprised and overwhelmed to see it on that screen, in that place.

NAME: VIVIANA YY

Aliases: Ondina

Age: 19 years.

Place of origin: Sy1, Fraction M24.

Specialty: Handling goldgun500, coppergun900 firearms

Languages: English, Spanish.

Killed victims:

- **Minister of International Relations: Clara Ramos de Terra.**
  - **Federal Recruitment Commissioner: Jaime Crest Riva.**

"I don't understand" she says "Does this mean that I will be the first to be executed?" Her face reflects genuine terror. She has the roundest pair of eyes I know, her light lashes, almost blonde like her hair, with her scar, her whole expression shows fear and it makes her face wrinkle.

"I doubt very much that this is a preamble to death" says Satiro, he tries to fix his hair, because lately it has been a mess, beautiful, but still a disaster, and that is something that a person like him cannot afford.

Ondina's image fades and Drider is projected onto the hologram. Unlike my friend, he does not move with ease in his image. He remains serious and spare, almost fed up, as if his hologram knows that we are observing him and is annoyed by it, his unreal self takes out a cigarette and lights it.

Name: Adolfo Caz M. M

Alias: Drider

Age: 21 years.

Place of origin: Sy4, Fraction M3.

Specialty: Handling of minimized stab (miniknife, miniblaze) and chemical knowledge to create poisons, grade 20, goldgun100.

Languages: English, German, Italian, Spanish.

Featured victims:

- **Secretary of Economy and Resources: Romeo Nep Ter.**
- **General Manager of The GREENLAND Telecommunication Company: Jessica Malone de Sanz.**

"Dr. Jessica was one of the fastest jobs I've ever had," says Drider, remembering almost wistfully, his minimal smile highlights the wickedness of his eyes, which, by the way, is attractive. I am even a bit jealous of Dr. Jessica, because when she died the last thing she saw were Drider's thin lips, but her image is erased and the next to be projected is Silfide. Unlike Drider, she seems to be in full modeling demonstration, her hologram smiles, winks, and even blows sporadic kisses. No one has ever questioned the perfection of her body and face but she likes to constantly show it.

"It's not my best angle," she says, and maybe it's just my impression, but her voice doesn't have the same security as always, rather it seems that she's looking towards someone with some doubt. Towards Satiro?

"You're crazy," says Ondina, already much more relaxed than a while ago. "You always honor your alias."

Name: Dulce Corr Yanz

Alias: Silfide

Age: 19 years

Place of Origin: Sy1, fraction 07

Specialty: Handling goldgun710, silvergun300 firearms and creation of chemical"biological poisons.

Languages: English, French, Spanish.

Featured victims:

- **Surgeon, chief doctor of the Sy5 Health Center: Jean Bonall Cruz**
- **General Director in Charge of The National Economy of SyanL: Sally Castern Zendejas.**
- **Deputy Director and Trial Lawyer of Sy1 Sector 17 for State Members: Maryana Cerc Lopez.**

"Weird, what refers to Jean Bonall was neither with the use of a firearm, nor with poison," she smiles.

"It's evident" Satiro intervenes with a weary voice, as if he were explaining the multiplication tables "that they are not going to put: Specialty in seduction and provocation of a car accident, Silfide"

My friend disappears from the projection and is replaced by Sátiro, who in the image wears a black suit with a blue tie, impeccable. Unlike the current Satyr who watches from the sofa, the one with the hologram has no dark circles and exhales attractiveness and masculinity, despite being only a projection.

"Do you always have to look like you are about to get married?" Asks Estirge.

"I can't help it, I was born with a star," he replies, shrugging. His information begins to appear.

Name: Jair Abella Tatchert.

Alias: Satyr

Age: 20 years

Place of origin: Sy1, fraction M17.

Specialty: Goldgun900, goldgun X30, coppergun20 firearm, micro and maximum type stab, high specialty in Chemistry and Criminalistics, foreign connections in Kaoy and LaGem.

Languages: French, English, Spanish.

Featured victims:

- **Senator General for National and Economic Laws: Mario Rom Soarez.**
- **Executive of the Content area of La Televisora MediaSy: Josephine Mark Del Pozo.**
- **SyanL Presidency Personal Doctor: Marlene Riva Riva.**

- **SyanL Executor of the Period 201"204: Ricky Spunttino.**

"Well, you have had very prominent victims" Drider tells him with obviousness, when the attractive image of Satiro disappears from the projection.

"And in fact some of them aren't in this list" he answers, biting his little finger, as usual.

"Who is not there, according to you?" Estirge looks at him in disbelief, constantly doubting everything Satiro affirms, especially his personal achievements.

Estirge has always been bothered by Satiro's conceit, and Satiro by Estirge's constant pretentiousness, but both have learned to live with it and regularly they end up bonding when Drider disparages them both. It is undoubtedly Satiro who has the greatest range of abilities, as this report has pointed out, not for nothing is the one who has the greatest number of relevant victims to his credit, however, on one occasion he was close to being captured, but Drider rescued him from. From that moment there are two memories that no one leaves behind: the thin scar that Satiro has from the lower abdomen to the crotch and Drider's sufficiency in reminding him that if it were not for him, he would be dead.

The image of Estirge is formed in the hologram, there he smiles and when I see him I realize that I have not seen that smile live for several days, the smile of complicity that I miss and that I did not know I missed until this moment.

Name: Jimmy Adkint T.

Aliases: Estirge

Age: 20 years

Place of origin: Sy4 Fraction F17

Specialty: Handling of firearms at all levels (gold, silver, copper) mastery of 4 martial arts (Karate, Taekwondo, Jiu Jitsu and kung fu).

Languages: German, English, Italian.

Featured victims:

- **Government Inspector of the Laws and Sanitary Regulations Area of La Nación: Jeremías Báez.**
  -General of the Police Force of State Guards: Marco Morales Roble.
  -Distributor of Class B methamphetamine in 5 fractions of Sy1: Maxi Falcone.

"Marco Morales has been the worst femicide in the history of SyanL" comments Sílfide, making a gesture of disgust. She's right, that guy murdered, raped, and tortured many Sy4 women, that's why Estirge used all the brutality he could against him, Morales had messed with his place of origin and not only his, Sy4 is also my home.

The image of the hologram changes and I am the one that appears in it, there I smile and make some faces, as if trying to remain serious. I don't know where they could get that image from.

"What was so funny?" Silfide asks me, referring to my laughing hologram.

"I have no idea."

"You look so pretty" that is the first soft expression that comes from Drider's mouth these last days. I look at him without thanking him, I don't know if this is the right time.

Name: Corina Ulloa AT

Alias: Gorgon.

Age: 19 years.

Place of origin: Sy4, fraction S30

Specialty: Handling goldgun900 long range firearm, handling miniblaze stab, miniknife.

Featured victims:

- **Director of Television Communication: Ray Mota Cric.**
- **NexPhonia Deputy Director: Irindia Infante Lomb.**

Languages: Spanish, English, Italian, French.

And just like that, my image disappears and the projection turns off.

"We should have escaped from here by now," says Drider, standing up as if he couldn't bear to sit for another minute.

"And go where, Drider?" Satiro questions him, leaning reluctantly on the back of his seat, totally opposed to the gesture of the first.

"Don't be ridiculous" Estirge intervenes "in case you didn't notice, we arrived here escorted by a whole flotilla of class A guards."

"If they haven't killed us until now, they will if we try to flee" says Ondina.

"Also, don't tell me you're not curious about all this" Satiro moves his hands theatrically, covering the entire office where we are.

It's when the door opens.

"With all of this i know now, everything inside of my head, it all just goes to show me how nothing I know changes me at all "

Blink 182.

Pure water from SyanL springs says the sky blue label on the plastic bottle that I pass from one hand to the other. I press it lightly with my thumb, looking for a rhythm, from a song that I have left in the past. Because even though time is ticking and I'm no longer twenty-three, I still haven't forgotten. I wouldn't have to, it's only been fifteen years, but every sound, every memory, every scream and every applause continues to echo in my head like the echo of a lonely drummer in any ordinary whiskey club, in SyanL.

My mind travels a long way, dotted with so many transformations that any human being would explode with them. I am not just any human being. Life has not given me the opportunity to be. The memories appear so suddenly as my eyes wander over the lush forest behind the hall window. The armored glass, as in every SyanL government building, allows me to have a broad view of the fields that surround it; It is not my favorite building, personally I prefer my office in the center of Sy1. That's where I was born, on Sy1. I grew up in the suburbs of the most populated sector of the country. I'm used to everything that refers to it: the climate, the tall and majestic buildings, his centrality. Although fifteen years ago all this did not impress me at all, on the contrary, It infuriated me to see the opulence in the system, I detested each crystalline or gray bricked building, typical of the capital. I wrote many songs despising the government of my country. At that time I would never have worn a sixty-nine thousand dollar black suit, nor would I have worn a purple glass watch, crystals for it taken from the LaGem Mountains. I never would have done it. I still remember each of those songs and I haven't stopped playing guitar, even though it's a solo act now. Either way, I always lived it like this. For me the bass and drums in the band were just accompaniments or preambles of royalty that the guitar will always have. Maybe that's why I slipped away from that world, from those late-night meetings in bars where only Oyrt's whiskey was served, the most vulgar and common in the nation; at this time it is no longer openly marketed because it tarnishes SyanL's image when it comes to whiskey. Reneé was the one who proposed that law when she was Commercial Advisor to the Senate, two years ago, when she had not yet taken the position of Executor. I remember that she took the podium, dressed in her usual elegance, looking at everyone except me, as if it annoyed her having to explain her reasons for that new commercial law, which, because it was her proposal, no longer required argumentation that endorse.

Even I was offended, I was barely a year as President and it somehow hurt me that she spoke so disparagingly about a whiskey I drank many times when I was an amateur musician. I felt that she knew it, that she intended to show me with that speech, that she was against me and that she supported the one who in the election had been my opposition candidate: Charles Tovar, son of the late Cesare Tovar, who had preceded me in the Presidency of SyanL. Reneé would not have been the only dissatisfied, but she was a very strong one. In any case, it turned out not to be so, because that same night, the most effective Commercial Advisor in recent times, entered my room in the Government Residence, with an authority that dazzled me and left me without options. She was on my side and she intended to be for a long time.

Not all the passion from my guitar days had been consumed when I entered the Directorate of Modern Culture and Heritage Restoration at SyanL. Not all my desire to feel was buried when I had my first promotion to Director General of the Department, a position that was granted to me by Cesare Tovar himself, although many still comment that his dementia was already advanced at that time and that therefore, he gave away positions and promotions to anyone. For me it was fine, I had achieved a position of Director with only twenty-seven years. Even though I was alone, it didn't matter, I would keep climbing. Cesare Tovar, as insane as he was, liked my kindness and sympathy.

"Smarmy" they used to tell me in Culture and Restoration, however they said it by giving me a pat on the back or with a wink, some women crossing their legs. Even so, it was not a blarney, old Cesare was a better person being a senile old man than he was in his adulthood. And I won not only him, but several members of the Senate. I did it by being kind, taking an interest in their politics and square lives, inviting them to dinner, supporting them in the hate campaigns that many media outlets carried out in the last days of Cesare Tovar's government.

I walk down the hall and the photo of the former president of the country smiles at me from one of the walls. I hear the plane landing a few meters from here, on the runway for this building. A message from Reneé flashes on my Nexus: "They are disoriented and scared, it will be easier than we thought."

I smile, I don't know yet if it's due to luck but everything always turns out to be simpler for me, more in my way, easier.

When I made public my intention to run for President of SyanL, I was sure that the entire government and the inhabitants would make fun of it, because even if the latter had no influence whatsoever in the election of the country's president, it did not mean that they could not express their displeasure or rejoicing.

It was a surprise, I accept it, although never in public, that sixteen of the twenty Heads of Department expressed their support for me, allying themselves with my campaign, even without knowing me. It was Charles Tovar or me. The SyanL Senate has fifteen members, of which ten voted in my favor.

Through the glass I see the group of *Animalium* get off the plane duly escorted. It seems incredible to me that people so young require so much security around them. Those innocent faces do not fit with the infinite list of crimes that are related to them. And those are not misdemeanors. They are all murders: men, women, young, old, with two things in common: all the victims of these young people were members of the government and all of them were walking shits. The precise kind of crap I used to sing against fifteen years ago. Then I had no other possibility, then the only thing I could do was to manifest myself in that way. My music was my only weapon, and yet today that I am president, my hands are tied by a stronger, thicker rope, so finding these guys is lucky.

What should I do with them?

I smile at my reflection in the glass: use them.

CHAPTER

8

President Daniel Delonge is a young man for his position. He is thirty-five but took office at thirty-one.

When he enters, he goes directly to his desk, escorted by 5 class A guards. Executor Reneé also enters and closes the door behind her.

"I will be concise kids and get to the point" he says.

Daniel Delonge is wearing an impeccable black suit and after pressing two buttons on his NexPad, we know that he is recording everything he is going to tell us.

Reneé points out 6 chairs in front of the desk. I notice that the president did not even say good morning to us, but why should he say good morning to a group of criminals?

"As you have seen, we have all the information and data that incriminate you all in such a way that as of today you will no longer have any decision-making power in your lives, with all the file that each of you carries there are two possible exits" before he speaks, I'm almost sure what he's going to say, I take a quick look at my companions, they have different ways of expressing their nervousness: Satiro bites his nails and Estirge his lips. Ondina's paleness contrasts with Silfide's flushed face. Drider moves his leg in an involuntary tic, and I ...

"One: you spend enough time in prison so that you will never see sunlight again, alone, without ever seeing another person's face again, eating what our prisoners eat, which I am sure the ladies will not find appropriate", I can almost see that he is smiling.

We all knew that this would come, that we could not flee forever, that we are murderers and that no matter how bad or corrupt our victims were, we had no right to ...

"What is the other option? "Asks Estirge and I don't know why he does it, it is an obvious answer. The president grins.

"Your execution would be scheduled tomorrow," he says. Ondina covers her mouth and stifles a little cry. For someone who is dedicated to killing, she is very afraid of dying. All six of us have the same fear, of finding on the other side the evil and angry souls that we sent there. The fear of dying was born from other deaths, and the only shield, we believe, is to send the shadowy image, many other corpses, before we introduce ourselves, and what better if all of them were walking shits.

They deserved it I think, and that gives me the courage to speak up.

"And what is the purpose of this, then? you parade our information in front of us and then you sit us here to tell us about the fate that awaits us, for what?" I look at Daniel Delonge directly, at his pale blue eyes, in his face the lips form a grimace similar to a smile, I don't like it, it is a mocking and determined gesture.

"I know what you have done" he says "we have always known, Reneé and I closely follow all your movements Miss Corina, what is your alias? Gorgona?" He looks at me with interest "Like the famous Medusa! Right? She turned men to stone at the first glance! Lethal with those beautiful brown eyes" he stops. Beside me I feel Estirge holding his breath.

"But if my knowledge of mythology does not fail me, poor Medusa suffered a lot" he looks at me with empathy "and I know that too" his eyes shine; it is not fair to try to erase the past and that a person like Daniel Delonge, kicked the memories in front of my face, damn president, a thousand times, he shouldn't have touched that subject, he shouldn't have gone so far back. He shouldn't have. Not my family.

"You said you would be concise, and I only hear the chattering," I say, moved by rage, if he's going to kill me, let him do it now. But no, he does the opposite of any gesture of death: he laughs.

"Watch your words" says Reneé, who does not like it at all. I ignore her, we all do, even the President, who, after sending me one last meaningful look, turns to all of us.

"The reason we go to the trouble of having you here is to give you a third option."

"We do not have money!" Ondina says, defensively. I wish she hadn't said anything, it makes us look like idiots, if there is something that Daniel Delonge's government has, they are resources, SyanL is a place that thanks to the production of Whiskey, has everything, despite the current crisis, in compared to its neighbors, except for Toot Nation.

"Don't be ridiculous, girl" Reneé says "the small fortune that you have raised with this *noble job*" you can see the sarcasm in her voice for kilometers.

She looks at Satiro while she speaks.

"It means nothing to us, although being illegally collected, it is evident that it is confiscated by the SyanL Nation. In other words, you are ruined."

"And at our disposal" completes Daniel Delonge.

"So? Why have us here?" Drider asks, he's getting impatient, I can see it in the way he blinks, as if the light bothered him.

"Don't think that we haven't noticed some details that are in the officials and businessmen of their respective resumes" explains Daniel "they were all corrupt and even cruel, you could say."

"What? *You could say?*" Estirge released suddenly "they were shit, each and every one" is the first time he has spoken in all this time.

"Silence!" Reneé shuts him up again. I don't know if it's worship or this woman has a thing for Daniel Delonge. And they dare to talk about corruption and influence peddling, it's funny.

"The deal is as follows" Daniel takes his Nexus and presses a button, on the screen where our information came out, a figure whom we know well is projected.

"In case you don't know, this is Lola Teheran, President of Toot. And although what I'm about to say is not in her official positions, she is also a fraudster and she is in collusion with the mob, she is the main responsible for which the SyanL Whiskey industry has drifted in recent year, opposite to what happens with Toot, that every day grows more as a nation, although its whiskey is mediocre, compared to ours" explains Daniel Delonge "Everything is very simple, do you understand?"

Of course we understand it, even before he says it, from the moment Lola's plump body and silver smile appeared in the projection. We understood.

"I want her dead" sentence Daniel Delonge "not only me, I know that every citizen of our nation wants her finished. And you will take care of that."

"And why would we do it?" Estirge's voice makes me feel alert, I can feel his anger, he doesn't kill because someone ordered him to, he has done it for money, for revenge. We always need a reason, and Daniel Delonge gives it to us:

"Because someone has to die, her or you, kids"

"I don't understand how you can be so at peace" I say to Silfide, she doesn't answer, she continues with her exercises for at least five more minutes.

Once she's done, she looks at me and wipes the sweat from her reddish hair with a small towel.

"They spared us," she says resolutely.

"They are sending us to kill the president of another country!" I reply, although I know that my complaint is ridiculous at first, but Silfide takes pleasure in reaffirming it.

"And? That's what we do, that's what we have dedicated ourselves to in recent years, where did your good soul suddenly come from?" She says. I look at her a little hurt by her words, which although true, leave me in silence.

"Look" she continues, moderating her previous aggressive tone a bit "Lola is the same type of *porcherie* that we are used to disappearing, and you know it."

"Yes, she may be, but" My mind flies fast to the days before, where I was prostrate and tied to a bed, hard and rough as granite, with my eyes covered.

My head projects all those fearful thoughts to me: to die, that my friends were about to die as well, that Silfide herself, or Estirge, were going to. I feel the weight in the pit of my stomach and I have to sit up.

"Now what?" She says, more annoyed than worried about me.

"Nothing that matters to you," I reply, if she can pretend to be angry, I'm also sick of her rudeness.

I walk down the hall and go to the room they assigned us. There are three beds, one of mine and the other two are Ondina's and Silfide's. They haven't returned our clothes to us and I don't think they will. From now on, the Delonge government and Reneé's instructions dictate everything from how to dress to what to eat. When I get to the room, I lock myself in the bathroom and take off the black sports outfit they gave us to train. It's already nine in the morning and we get up at six thirty to exercise. According to Reneé, we are skilled and accurate, but in recent days we have become weak, although she did not specify that it was thanks to the beatings that her Class A Guards gave us when they captured us. That is why we have a week to prepare physically during the morning.

"In the afternoons you will dedicate time to study Lola; with my advice, you will elaborate the necessary plan to reach her" she had explained.

"Does it mean that you…" Ondina's voice had problems structuring her questions in front of Reneé "you will accompany us in the mission. "

"No" the Executor had answered "neither I nor anyone from the government can go with you, the SyanL Nation cannot and should not be involved in this, is that clear?"

And yes, it is very clear. I think about it, now that the hard drops of warm water wet my face and the bathroom begins to fill with steam and contrary to the haze formed here, I can clearly see Delonge and Reneé's plans: We are going to kill an enemy of our president, if we succeed, we return to SyanL to our old life, but if something goes wrong and the Toot government discovers us, we are alone in this, because we are murderers, outcasts, we are not recognized as people of our own state. If we are successful, that's good, if not, nobody will care, because nobody cares about us. The face of Estirge, when he smiled, crosses my mind, I do care about him and not only him, the rest of my friends as well.

I can hear the voices of Silfide and Ondina, they are already in the room. They will serve us breakfast only at half past ten and then we must meet with Reneé at eleven to work out the plan where my friends and I are instruments of no importance to anyone.

Daytime clothes are no better than training clothes: pants a bit loose and a jacket, both black. The t-shirt we wear is white without any kind of distinctive.

I still don't understand what place this is; In the morning we were in the gym and now I enter the dining room, which is huge, there are about fifty white rectangular tables, with chairs just as cold. It looks like a hospital cafeteria, yet all the tables are empty except one and that's where I'm headed.

He doesn't see me, I can see his back and his messy brown hair that would tell me from a thousand kilometers that it's him. He wears the same outfit as me.

"Estirge" I say sitting down in front of him. The chair makes a metallic noise when moved that spreads all over the place like nails on a blackboard. For a few moments we just looked at each other, analyzing our clothes and our faces.

"That color suits you well," he says.

"I didn't know whether to choose this or the yellow flower dress," I reply, he laughs suddenly, as if the same laugh surprised him.

"It is true that there are not many options, right?

"No, there aren't, but I guess I don't feel like choosing anything either" I look around "What place is this?

"From what I have heard" Estirge always listens "it is a training center for Class B and C Guards, but they have sent them away, for now there are only us, those who guard us and apparently that cook" he points towards the door, a thin man dressed in white approaches and without saying anything he puts six plates on the table. Estirge and I looked at each other.

"Eh ... the others haven't arrived yet" points out my friend. The waiter / cook shrugs and after putting the six servings on the table, he leaves. Minutes later he reappears with six glasses and a jug of natural water.

"Estirge" I say in a low voice once the waiter leaves again "I want to get out of here, I don't want to do this anymore" I whisper slowly, as if I wanted to make sure of what I'm saying. He passes saliva and I see that his eyes move from side to side, as if looking for an answer to give me on the flat white walls that surround us or on the perfectly arranged tables. He looks at me and I don't know why I feel even more afraid when he takes my hand in his. He has many ways of looking, many of them false or self-centered, he may have killed many people, but inside he is just a scared kid, like me, and that one is the look he has now.

"There is no way to run away, we can't take a risk, I don't want you to die trying" he says, his hands are cold "this time I do not want anyone to die" the noise that comes from the door makes him separate his hands from mine , the others have already arrived, they come closer and sit next to us. Every time I look at Ondina, it is hard for me to get used to the scar that she now shows on the side of her face.

I don't want anyone to die, the phrase repeats itself in my head throughout the day.

CHAPTER

eleven

"The biggest complication you will find to eliminate Lola is knowing her location. She is never in the same place two days in a row, she knows that many people are looking for her and not precisely to kiss her", Reneé explains, she is standing, taking occasional turns at the table where we are sitting. It is a long, oval table that has the same neatness and luxury as the rest of the place. Reneé wears a dark blue suit that must cost more than what we earned killing the four beetles.

This morning they gave each of us a NexusPhone, where we took notes of what Reneé tells us, the devices are equipped with the necessary applications, place, hours, weather, records of inhabitants, etc. As she explains, images that support what she indicates are projected in the center of the table.

"That is why" she says "the mission should be carried out in a single day, in the whiskey exhibition that is schedule in Toot and of which we will talk later, nonetheless, remember: a single day, maximum two, but that would be speaking of an extreme like the death of any of you" she comments mechanically.

"That's impossible" Satiro leaves his Nexus reluctantly and even roughly over the blue glass surface of the table "Do you have any idea how complex it can be?" he says to Reneé.

"Watch your tone" she holds his icy and impenetrable gaze; she has the power to send him cut into pieces and make a necklace with them. Satiro knows it and he keeps provoking her. I would like to say that I do not understand it, but the reality is that I do, I know it too well.

"The idea is the same: it is impossible to search, find, kill Lola and escape in a single day, don't you see?

"He's right" Silfide seconds him "we don't know Toot as we know SyanL, she is hiding and surely she has the maximum protection of her government, guards of the highest class that follow her everywhere."

"And in the remote possibility of finding her and outwitting her guards, do you think that Lola doesn't have at least basic training?" Ondina ends the statement. It's the first time I've heard her speak confidently these days. Her loose blond hair falls over her face to cover the scar, yet it is still damaged by the eternal blemishes of acne.

Reneé exhales, annoyed with our complaints, she doesn't like having to socialize with us, after all, we are exactly what she wants to eliminate from SyanL: a group of murderers.

"I thought you had the experience that your history mentions" she looks at us, her eyes stop at me, "but I see that you are nothing more than a group of spoiled brats, bored with the family fortune you once had."

Again. My throat starts to burn, the way it feels when a difficult, painful, and embarrassing memory is brought before your face.

"Look who's talking" Estirge murmurs, his face flushed, as red as if he had drunk a liter of whiskey in one gulp. Reneé glares at him and then turns to the guard behind Estirge.

"This one," she says, almost with pleasure, the guard puts the fine golden weapon pointing to Estirge's forehead.

"NO! PLEASE!" I shout, getting up, I can't, another guard holds me and points at me too. Ondina is the next one trying to get up, but Reneé's voice prevents her.

"Not a move or you all die," she says. My friends look at her with hatred, my body trembles as if it had been in the rain for days. I hate Reneé crossing her arms and looking at Estirge like that, I hate her thin lips spitting out the words that will give me nightmares for the next days.

"I am not like you, I have always done what I have to do, regardless of the sacrifices" she looks at us "that one is the only advice you will receive from me" she says. After a long silence, she looks at her guards "let's go."

When they release me, I hasten to hug Estirge and I can hear Reneé's voice:

"Stupid kids."

CHAPTER

12

"I'd kill her" says Silfide, walking down the hall, in front of us.

"You know?" replies Drider, who on the contrary, comes behind the rest "that verb begins to lose meaning."

"Which one? *Kill*?" Satiro asks, stopping and looking at him.

"Yes, *kill*" he answers "no longer scares, no longer causes chills or disgust, or tremors, it is already a place more than an action, and one not too far by the way, from there is no coming back" he says, his eyes look darker than usual.

We walk towards the rooms still with rage on the skin, Estirge remains silent, hands in pockets, staring at the floor.

"See you guys tomorrow" Silfide says goodbye to them, yawning. Having been with Reneé for ten hours in a row is exhausting. Nobody feels like talking. Satiro waves goodbye to us and opens the door to the adjoining room.

"*Corina*" says Drider, it startles me to hear my real name, I see that Estirge finally raises his eyes and looks at us "Can I talk to you for a moment?" Drider continues "Alone?" He emphasizes the word when he sees that Ondina looks at us with curiosity. I nod, he walks over but doesn't say anything until everyone enters the rooms. I watch as the hallway lights hit his wristwatch, where he bears the symbol of the black widow.

"Yesterday I woke up after midnight, it was not cold. When I opened my eyes I was scared, I looked around and I was half asleep, awake, I don't know, I was not sure, but I dreamed that you ..." he takes me by the shoulders, I am sure of what he will say "that you didn't get to…" and I want him to shut up, because his words can cause me real fear, a fear that I don't need right now.

"It was a nightmare" I say, I would take his hand, I would hug him, but I can't, my hands feel cold, my arms are asleep.

"Yes, but it made me see reality" he puts his hands on my cheeks, his touch is trembling, and his fear is contagious "you must go."

"Go away? Where? What are you talking about?" I stutter, in part I think he is joking but his serious face indicates that he is not. Suddenly I forget the fear and I want to hit his nose with all the force of my fist. Is he an idiot?

"I have thought about it all day, this building is a military shelter, there must be a secret exit, a way to escape, all the shelters in SyanL have it and this is no exception, I have thought that"

"I don't want to leave," I say, hoping my gaze makes it clear.

"You're in danger here!"

"We all are in danger! The six of us are in the same situation!" I raise my voice as he has already done it.

"You have to understand, Gorgona!" Suddenly he speaks slowly again "it's for your good."

"How do you think that I could leave like this?" I take a breath and try to speak in a lower voice "leaving you guys here?

"You can't even imagine my nightmare" he says, putting his hands over his ears, as if he wanted to cover up the noise that the dream still makes. I feel guilty, the only thing Drider wants is to protect me, all I do is lower my gaze, the same action I always do in these situations, he takes my hand and lowers his voice even more.

"Come on, we must plan your escape, but you should not tell anyone, because there will be someone who suggests that we all go and-"

"I'm not going anywhere" I stop him emotionless "we are here together, we have all done the same type of crimes and we all are all going to kill Lola, she is the only pass to freedom we have."

"I don't want you to die" he says, no longer arguing. It's strange, we've been making so many risky plans together for many years and he had never told me this so clearly. I would like to tell him that it will not happen, that he must have confidence, that everything will be fine, but I only say something that comes scratchy from my throat.

"I don't want to die either."

CHAPTER

13

It's a bird that wakes me up, but I don't open my eyes instantly. The alarm hasn't gone off and I can hear Ondina and Silfide's breaths on the beds next to mine. Outside the bird continues singing, it must be almost five in the morning. I snuggle under the covers, I would like to stay here like this, comfortable and warm, without having to face any training, or Reneé's insults.

I try to imagine that he is by my side, out of all danger, that his hair is ruffled by the pillow I try to imagine that he never leaves.

I squeeze my eyelids as if wanting that moment to last, even if it's not even real.

The alarm clock on the night table rings, the bird outside is no longer singing and the image of him next to me, which I built with my eyes closed, is not there either.

I open my eyes and realize that it is already dawn.

We are not allowed to go out at all. We have days without breathing the clear air, we see the sunlight through the windows and the stars in the same way. Every day we have the same breakfast, lunch, and dinner, but at each meal, we drink a kind of smoothie that is supposed to give us energy. It tastes like spicy oil to me, but I still drink it. Satiro is the only one who seems to enjoy it.

"It brings back memories of home, the chef is from my fraction in Sy1, where this energy drink was created, my mother used to prepare it for my father every day, but he did not like it" Satiro seems to remember clearly, he even smiles when he says it "and I drank it because my brother-"

"It tastes like the liquid that comes in tuna cans" Silfide interrupts, making a very exaggerated gesture of disgust, as if she were going to vomit, Satiro looks at her, it seems that this comment hurts him, but immediately recovers his confident semblance.

"At least I have a memory of my childhood" he answers smiling and it's a low move. Silfide doesn't have a single beautiful thought about her own childhood, she doesn't even know who her parents were, she was in a shelter called "The

Army of Saviors" until she was fourteen and was able to escape. She always tries to say so little about it, and when she does, she despises the sour food and dirty water in that place, not to mention the old, threadbare blanket where she used to sleep.

Instantly, Satiro realizes that this time he has crossed the line, she looks at him and stands up, leaving the dining room.

"How sensitive, Satiro" says Estirge "next time you should tell her that you did have your parents at family festivities"

"She started" he responds, drinking the last of his glass, only I realize that he grabs Silfide's one and drinks it too.

"The truth is that she has a point" comments Ondina with a barely audible voice "first I thought they wanted to poison us."

"Don't be silly" says Satiro, I know he feels guilty and that makes him, wanting to get even so he could feel better "Why would they want to poison us if they have everything on their favor to execute us in public?"

"Don't take it with Ondina either," says Estirge. Suddenly I want Satiro to keep making her look like an idiot and I join to the conversation.

"But it's true" I say, Ondina looks at me confused and then looks at Estirge, incredulous, as if she was looking for his words to defend her, that angers me more. "I mean, it is true that poisoning does not make sense" I finish, "it is absurd."

"Thank you", Satiro winks at me "beautiful, intelligent ... and maliciously" he glances at Estirge and then at me again, "what does someone like you need, *Corina*?", apparently everyone has the sudden desire to call me by my real name.

"She needs to be sensible about certain things" says Drider, who until now had been silent, I know very well why he says that it's about our talk the other day, when he told me I should escape.

"What do you mean?" Estirge asks, but there is no time to chat, a guard comes to tell us that Reneé is waiting for us in the projection room.

"Gorgona?" Ondina takes my arm as we walk towards the room, we have already taken off our training attire and again we look like young lawyers with those black suits. "Are you angry with me?", she looks me in the eye, her round face and her blond hair, if we were mythology, she would look like a mermaid, as its alias says, although on the other hand, mermaids are not necessarily beautiful.

"Of course not" I answer, but I let go of her arm under the excuse of removing some strands of hair from my face "why do you say that?"

"I don't know, it gave me that impression a while ago in the dining room, when you sided with Sátiro and all that", she says, I wish she would lower her voice, Silfide turns around and looks at me with surprise, as if I had betrayed her.

"I did not side with anyone" I say, also high enough so that Silfide listens, "this is not about sides, Ondina, on the contrary, this is not the school to walk taking sides, we are all together in this horrible business."

"Are you sure?" She asks me, insisting, her lips tremble when she says something that makes everyone stop around me. "Are you sure you haven't thought of abandoning us? I don't want you to abandon us" she concludes. I feel four pairs of eyes on me, the only one that doesn't seem surprised is Drider.

"No!" I answer at last, about to get angry. "Where do you get that from?" I look at Ondina and then at Drider, sure he commented. Or at least that's what I believe before hearing it.

"I heard you" a barely visible tear runs down his cheek "sorry, but I heard you talking to Drider the other day, forgive me, forgive me Gorgona, I don't want you to leave, don't leave me here!" she says and hugs me, she's crying openly, and I feel the guilt that Satiro must have felt a while ago.

"Then you should also have listened" Drider gets into the conversation, separates us and, staring at her, points at her "you should have heard yourself, that Gorgona said that she will not go anywhere, that she does not want to leave us and that she refused my proposal.

"Quiet" Satiro also intervenes, stepping in the middle "calm down, Drider, everything is ok" but despite his attempts, Ondina looks upset and responds almost immediately.

"But I don't know, *we* don't know if you and Gorgona have other *secret meetings*, I don't know if you've talked to her in other occasions, I don't know if you've convinced her, I don't know if she said yes!" She looks at him with a certain anger and her eyes are red, her tears do not stop coming out, one after another, her red mouth has also swollen a little.

"Let's see" Silfide speaks too, just as upset. "How wonderful! could it be that with this union we can go for Lola and be successful?... This is absurd, no one is going anywhere. NO ONE. It's impossible, Reneé doesn't have any security flaws in this building, she can't risk one of us going on a trip to Toot to tell Lola that six killers are after her plump body full of stretch marks, is that clear?" Silfide speaks firmly and I see Drider nods, resigned that his initial plan regarding me has been foolish. But then, as if a bee had stung me, I discover what is bothering me so much at this moment: his silence.

"What about you? You don't say anything?" My lips are dry, Estirge shrugs and twists his mouth indifferently.

"I don't know, stay, go, do what you like" and just like that, he goes to the projection room where surely Reneé is very angry waiting for us. Drider and Satiro follow him. I don't know why, but I feel that with those words the subject is finished, that if someday someone reopens it, it can only be him.

"Definitely the worst day since we got here," says Silfide. She takes me by the shoulders "are you okay? "

And the truth is that I am not because I know that with this type of episodes, they will kill us at the precise moment we step on Toot.

I'm not, because Estirge doesn't care if I leave or stay here. I'm not because he suddenly looks at me like if those childish scenes are my fault. I'm not, I want to drink something strong, whiskey from SyanL, a glass of *Joan Megghia* that will sink into my throat and seal it like a candle seals the iron, so that it won't let me say what I want to say. I am not, I wish my history of taken lives could be erased as in the records of the home Nexus. I am not because I know that we are going to die and I am not because I no longer want to kill anyone, not even Lola.

"Yes, I'm OK."

"Come on" Silfide smiles at me and walks towards the projection room.

"Gorgona?" Ondina says to me again, I look at her, "please, don't ever abandon us. Without you this mission is a failure" she says before walking after Silfide. I think of her words, but later I remember those of Estirge, I think it is rather the other way around, that this mission, with me, will be a failure.

"Today I will give you the most important explanation and you have the luxury of being late and wasting your time and worse, mine," says Reneé. It doesn't surprise me anymore, it's her role. Or I don't know if it is, but she's doing amazingly well.

"Anyway, you don't ask for pears from the elm," she continues, resigned. I do not understand her, if we are as useless as she says every time she has a chance, why us? "I need you to pay attention and ask all the questions you consider necessary, even if they seem absurd and I think they will be" she squints at time she presses the screen of her Nexus.

The figure of a fat man, half bald, with a lofty suit, but not enough to hide his bulging stomach is projected before us like that day our own images were presented, with the history of crimes of each one of us. The fat man in the projection smokes and runs his hand through his thinning hair, as if he were an attractive man.

"This is Ramón de Barbé", explains Reneé, "he is President of Toot's General Communications Network and

General Manager of TootVision, as well as a majority shareholder of InterToot."

"Uffa, and by any chance he doesn't sell chocolates outside the cinema, too?" Satiro teases, Reneé glares at him before continuing. She is not in the mood for my friend's comments.

"It is true that Ramón de Barbe is a man very involved in his work, he does not have a close family, more than a few nephews, he lives with a woman, but the reports really show that Barbé's life is centered on his jobs. He is one of the people they have to go through to get to Lola", explains Reneé. The projection below shows a map.

"Ramón will be simple, he may be an ally of Lola, but our informants indicate that he seeks power for himself, so any attempt to remove Lola from the middle will be well received by him.

"Is he Lola's henchman?" I ask, Reneé nods.

"Yes and one of the most powerful men of Toot."

"And why not establish some connection with him? An alliance?", asks Estirge, his mouth moves with confidence, he seems very concentrated.

"That is out of the table, we are not going to eliminate Lola to leave the way for someone even worse and Ramón is certainly worse than Lola."

"So?" Estirge looks confused.

"Then you kill Ramón. Period."

"Is he the only person who could be an obstacle?" Asks Ondina taking notes on her Nexus.

"No" Reneé answers, "although he is a very important part of the plan, since the mission will take place in his residence, during a Whiskey Exhibition Gala that he will offer and to which Toot's crème de la crème are invited. You will sneak in."

In the projection a new image appears, he is a young man, no older than thirty years, tall with dark green eyes, wavy hair and, as can be seen, perfect teeth within a perfect smile. He wears a smart gray suit, but he looks for some reason more carefree than the last, to tell the truth, he is close to being the most attractive guy I have ever seen and apparently I am not the only one who thinks so.

"Oh baby... Who is he?", Silfide asks, I can't help but laugh. Reneé looks at us as if she were the teacher who reprimands two students by whispering.

"His name is Alex Zendejas, he is President of the National Bank of Toot, he personally manages practically all the accounts of the important people of that country, as well as that of the State itself. Ramón de Barbé trusts Alex, Lola trusts him in the same way, because he keeps track of their financial accounts, however, Alex Zendejas will not be the only man of great confidence for Lola who also attends the Gala."

"Then *Alex*," says Satiro "is good for three shits. He's a nobody."

"Yes," Estirge completes, "he looks useless."

"We could just eliminate him, right? Even if it is not the only one," Drider concludes. And speaking of school behaviors, these three, jealous of a potential enemy.

"You will have to eliminate him", Reneé clarifies, "I do not project him here just to be able to admire his beautiful face" she says and her always sour voice sweetens a bit, surely the *beautiful face* part she has said it because it is inevitable to think about it.

"Alex Zendejas has much importance in Lola's cabinet, since he is the direct manager of Toot's finances and commercial system, that includes whiskey productions" Reneé removes Alex's image, "however, in all of Toot there is no dog more faithful to Lola than the head of security."

"I know who he is, I've seen him on the net", mentions Estirge, "Luis Romano, right?"

"Well, at least someone of you takes the trouble to investigate," Reneé smiles at him, pressing a button that makes Alex's figure disappear and projects a short, gray-haired man dressed in black, with a Nexus in his hands, who at first glance, doesn't look threatening, however I have learned that those are the worst.

"This, as your partner already mentioned, is Luis Romano, a very dangerous man who would give his life and the life of his own family in order to protect Lola.

"Yes, he is the right arm of the president of Toot", affirms Estirge.

"Uhm ... I have a question" I say and I know that it will probably sound absurd, but I have to do it, "is it absolutely necessary to kill the three of them?", I pass saliva at the end of my question, Reneé looks at me incredulously, "I mean… it is Lola whom we want, right?", I finish. Reneé crosses her arms and seems to reunite patience before answering me.

"Wait…dear *Gorgona*, are you softening?", she asks me. I look at the table, then at the image of Luis Romano, and finally at Estirge.

"No", I answer, "but if we leave a trail of a slaughter like that, of the most important figures of Toot, Lola will know immediately that we are going for the big shot that she is, the World Council of Peace will suspect something", I finish and look up to meet her eyes, proud of my own argument, but she puts her hands on her face in annoyance, as if she no longer can stand the ineptitude that I apparently distill with each word.

"I had already told you that this should be done in a single day, right? In the Gala that Ramón de Barbé will organize", she looks at me as if I were stupid and then I dare to raise my voice, putting the Nexus in front of her at the same time. "Lola is our main objective, but the chaos that will be unleashed with her death must be increased with the complete collapse of her cabinet of henchmen.

"Do you know how quickly this device can transmit news and events?", My voice comes out higher than I would have liked, while I point at it with my Nexus. Reneé raises her index finger in front of my eyes, for a moment it seems to me that she will hit me, but it doesn't.

"First: I have warned you: DON'T TALK TO ME LIKE THAT!", she exclaims. Nobody says anything and she continues, now with a more moderate voice, "and second: you partner *Adolfo…Drider*, will be in charge of deactivating the system just before starting the operation, with this it will be complicated, but not impossible, that there will be visual evidence at the Gala, an it will be even more unlikely that the images are sent to the World Peace Council, you will however not lose any connection because you will be in communication with SyanL's network, not Toot's."

"In other words, will we have to kill all four of them at the same time?", Satiro asks.

"We are talking about the leaders in Finance, Communication and Security of the Toot nation, obviously their enemies are growing in numbers, I do not doubt that there will be several of them at that gala, I am pretty sure that every day they know their heads are in risk. We must trust that."

"Trust?", says Silfide, incredulous, "so at the end of the day, our mission is based on trust?", she has that feline gesture that she makes when she gets angry, she is holding back so as not to explode.

"Everything has its risk", Reneé answers without flinching, "you know it very well", she smiles, damn bitch.

"I understand that", Estirge begins, his clear and almost sarcastic voice fills the room, "but what happens later? Suppose we succeed and we get to Lola without problem, suppose everything goes according to plan and we kill her."

"I like your attitude, *Jimmy*," Reneé interrupts, I can almost swear that she smiles at him with a certain flirt. Bitch, calling him by his real name.

"What happens next, Reneé?", He continues speaking without paying attention to her ridiculous poses. "How will we get out of Toot? How will we get back to SyanL?"

"There will be a jet waiting for you, we will track your location."

"A SyanL jet?" I ask, Reneé looks at me again, belittling my question with her gesture.

"Obviously not, girl", she says jaded, then explains "it will be a black-market jet, we cannot risk with an official vehicle."

"But… no", Silfide finally says what we all think "what happens if the jet doesn't arrive? What happens if it is intercepted or shot down?" She looks at Reneé, my friend's expressive eyes full of fear and resignation at the same time.

"Again guys, we will have to trust. After all, a group of assassins must have some kind of friendship with luck, right?"

CHAPTER

17

I knock hard on the bedroom door, as if the three of them had to pay it to me, as if the three of them had made me feel this way.

But I must do it today, tomorrow we go to the Coast, then to Toot and during the whole journey I will not be able, much less during the mission.

It is Satiro who opens the door, wearing only jeans and as always, he has no shame in not wearing a shirt, even if we find ourselves in this situation.

"I need to talk to Estirge," I say, crossing my arms, with a hard tone of voice, I try not to see his abdomen, which is actually quite nice.

"Talk or slap him?" He jokes, but I'm not in the mood for that, it seems that Satiro understands it quickly. "Estirge, someone is looking for you! Don't you want to come in?" He asks me.

"No thanks."

"What is it?" Estirge is already in the doorway, next to Satiro.

"I need to talk with you."

"Here I am" a disheveled Estirge with a sleepy face appears in front of me.

"Will you join me for a walk?" I say, Satiro looks at us and frowns and then returns to the interior of the room. Estirge comes out and closes the door behind him.

We walk down this hallway that looks like a huge, endless gray cube. Suddenly what I rehearsed in my head all afternoon is not so easy to say.

"What do you want to talk about?" He asks me as if this was a normal day, as if it were not tomorrow the day we embark on what undoubtedly resembles a collective suicide.

"Do you remember the mission we had before they caught us?" I say, he smiles, walks with his hands in his pockets, it seems like I'm asking him about his last birthday and not about a cold-blooded murder.

"Of course, it was what put us here: the executor."

"Yes, that's what I mean, the moment I shot him" I start, Estirge looks at me and puts his hand on my shoulder, I ignore the gesture and everything I feel with it.

"There is no reason for you to feel responsible that they have caught us, I was there too and well, it is true that Drider was also a participant in it", his voice disperses a bit, as if diminishing importance. I don't know if he is trying to take off importance to Drider or the murder itself.

"No, I do not feel guilty, in fact that is what I want to tell you: the moment I shot him, when he fell to the ground, when we fled and even on the way to the airport that day, I did not feel any guilt, nor with the others I ever eliminated" I stop before continuing, "they deserved it."

"I totally agree" he answers.

"But" and then I finally let go of what has been torturing me for days before going to bed, "Lola deserves it?", He narrows his eyes, as if searching with extreme care for an answer, he even bites his lip, as when he is nervous.

"I don't know if Lola deserves it, and I'm not just talking about dying, but about leaving her nation in complete helplessness, without a leader, open to revolts and civil war, as happened 19 years ago, before she came to power. Toot is a small country, much smaller than SyanL, but in the last two decades they have shown a financial and commercial productivity of almost eighty percent, I mean it is true that their whiskey does not even reach the shoes of SyanL, however without their president, they will collapse, there is no doubt. That little they have achieved in this time, will go to waste."

"That's what I mean, the victim is not only her, it is Toot, it will be as if each citizen received the blow, citizens like us ... citizens like we were once, many years ago" I explain, he nods and looks at me concerned, with that expression I've seen so many times.

"It won't get you anywhere to think about it."

"I know! And it's not that I'm *softening* as Reneé said, but do they deserve it? Do the people of Toot deserve it? You better than anyone know that I am not a supporter of the Toot government, you know that I always speak shit of them when it comes to whiskey, but this? Is this what we should do? I don't know if there is a less harsh way to put it, do they deserve it?" I look for an answer in his pupils, but they look different, far from to this moment, far away.

"Deserve? *Deserve* is one of those words that for me lost their meaning since… many years ago, when my mother abandoned me and I was two days old. I do not know with certainty the whole story between my father and her, he was never clear about it, he only told me that she had left, that she could not and did not want to take care of me, that I was not the type of child she could love, surely as an adult I would lack many things ... and why? I was just a baby, a healthy and innocent baby, I was two fucking days old!", he says and turns to me, as if I were that mother with a blurred face who he tries to erase it from his head, "did I deserve it, Corina? Did I deserve it !?" he says, pointing himself to emphasize his gesture. I don't know what to say to him, I'm silent and so is he. The only thing I do because I don't feel capable of more is put my hand on his shoulder, like he did just some moments ago. His shoulder tenses in that instant, with that caress.

"That's life, Gorgona, you should know it well" he says at last "and I think of us", for a moment I think he refers to him and me, but not "the six of us, looking for the worst, not only these days, but always ... Satiro and Silfide with their dramas or Drider and their daily complaints about everyone, or Ondina who cries if you tell her that your head hurts, I think about that and", he looks at me "we always seek the worst, and know? Difficult times come, we don't have to search them."

And then I don't have to hug him because he is the one who does it, nor can I tell him that I am afraid of losing him and that, that is the main reason that moves me: fear of losing him forever.

Reneé has tried hard to be annoying since she first saw us. But what's worse, she likes to be that kind of person and shows off it whenever she gets a chance.

"I don't have friends and I'm very well," she had responded to Ondina in a session where she told us what to do in an emergency. The first rule was to run away and the second to keep your mouth tightly shut.

"And our mates?", had been Ondina's question, "How could we leave them?", The answer had been just as clear, Reneé does not retain any friendship. And I believe her, clearly it is seen that President Delonge is enough for her.

Sílfide thinks she is gold digger and climber, she may be right, but there is something that in Reneé never fails: her organization. And that's what allows us to create a well-designed plan to get to Toot without any suspicions. We left yesterday and we haven't traveled directly to Toot. We go to the Coast first as it was the plan when we wanted to escape, before all this started. This is how Reneé had put it.

"You will stay two days on the coast, then, separated by schedules and in different transport routes, you will travel to Toot, on Tuesday. At nine o'clock in the morning Jair and

Viviana will travel, by train, the travel information is in the folders: order, tickets, etc ...”

“Train?”, Satiro had said rolling up his eyes “from the coast to Toot, are we going to travel by train? Five hours?”, He looked at Reneé with obvious annoyance.

"I'm not going to waste time with such idiotic questions," she answered without looking at him. "Adolfo and Dulce travel by bullet train at three in the afternoon, they will be arriving in Toot at approximately six in the afternoon."

Silfide had looked at me without holding back. Drider has always seemed sullen, boring, and demanding to her. He surely would not talk during the trip and criticize everything she did.

“Jimmy and Corina will travel at ten o'clock at night, by plane” Reneé had informed, I opened the folder with the travel documents, at least he was going to be with me and we could continue talking. Traveling with Estirge did bother me at all on what could be the last trip of my life. I hoped he was thinking the same thing as me, but he was studying his folder carefully until Reneé said something that made him turn and me too.

“Corina and Jimmy will travel at the same time, but on a different plane.”

"What? Why?" I looked at her with the intention of throwing the folder to her face. She had looked at me, pursing her lips, as if stifling a smile before speaking:

"I said I wouldn't answer stupid questions."

"Because beggars and murderers have the most interesting stories", says Satiro on the plane, I'm sitting next to him, we're just a few minutes from landing on La Costa. He puts milk in his cinnamon tea, unlike Estirge, he never drinks coffee.

"I asked you if you're not nervous or worried," I say in a low voice making sure no one is listening.

"That's why I'm not, I've always wanted my life to be an interesting story and it's on the way to be," he says and raises his hand to get the attention of the flight attendant, who immediately approaches.

"Sir?" The brunette with very wide hips and a tiny waist smiles at him, the whiteness of her teeth contrasts with her skin, it reminds me of the models of the ancient republic of Africa, a very classic type of beauty that is of fashion lately. Satiro loves that kind of beauty.

"I'm going to need more sugar, sweetheart" he winks at her, I've seen that gesture so many times that in this very moment, I find it annoying so I take his hand and look at the flight attendant innocently.

"My husband shouldn't eat so much sugar anymore, Miss, don't bring us anything please" I smile and put my hand on Satiro's leg, she looks at me uncomfortably and leaves.

"What the hell Gorgona? If I die, you will carry the guilt of taking away my last moment of happiness."

"Don't be silly" I remove my hand and clear my throat "I want to talk to you and I don't need someone with long legs to distract you" he takes a small drink of his tea, he wears a suit like the ones he usually wears and a small hat that looks like something from the most exclusive stores in Kaoy, the quintessential fashion specialist nation.

"Talk about what?"

"Well, you know that it is not easy" suddenly I do not know how to say it "everything is very complicated ... our safety, knowing if we will be fine or not ... or as you said!, tomorrow maybe ..."

"Alright" he stops me "I know what you mean and I know what you'll say" he looks at me as he continues stirring the tea with the silver spoon.

"You know? Thank goodness, I want to ask you, as friends, please, Satiro.."

"No" he says and continues drinking his tea.

"No? How could you say no? I haven't even told you what I'm talking about" I answer, Satiro looks me straight in the eyes.

"You want me to watch someone's back, right?" The sound of the spoon with the cup resounds more than it should. Estirge turns from a couple of seats in front and raises his eyebrows, as if asking if there is a problem. Satiro smiles at him with the friendliness of a grandmother and raises his cup of tea as if toasting. He turns to me again, still looking at Estirge's back.

"And I know who you have in mind" he warns, I feel embarrassed but that doesn't matter to him.

"Will you?" I insist, although he has already given his answer. Satiro licks a bit of the sugar residue on the spoon, he doesn't look at me, his eyes look distant, absorbed in something else. I know they go back to the memory of a restaurant, to a business dinner.

"If you see any Guards class A vehicle, give me the signal and we will leave here, for the B and C do not worry, I have them all bought"

And that was always the point at which Satiro stopped when telling that story. He had failed the most important person in his life, years ago.

"No."

"Why not?" I beg, I won't give up so easily.

"I have already promised that I would take care of someone else," he answers, placing the cup on the folding table.

"Take care of who?

"Of you"

CHAPTER

20

At eleven in the morning, we landed on the coast. Satiro next to me looks flawless, clean skin and wavy hair in order. My own hair looks like a used scouring pad and my skin glows disgustingly. Before Satiro wakes up, I wipe my face with a handkerchief. The rest of my friends, each one in their seat, have already woken up. Silfide dressed like she's ready for a workout routine drinks a pasty-looking green liquid.

We will spend two days at the beach but we cannot leave the hotel.

"Are you going to tell me who asked you to watch my back?" I ask Satiro, he yawns shaking his head and puts a hand on my face, hopefully he doesn't notice that my face is oily from the sleep.

"No, I'm sorry, I'm a vault."

When we get off the plane I feel the warm breeze on my face, the heat of the coast is very unique. It is always cloudy, the sun does not come out and sometimes it rains for weeks, but the heat does not stop, whatever happens. They don't know what cold is. But we are used to SyanL which is a place full of all climates, which is why it is so easy to have good whiskey at home. But the inhabitants of the coast have never felt the steam rising from their mouths when they exhale on a day covered in icy clouds, they have never tasted the warmth of a blanket on a frozen night.

We are among the many tourists who come to the Coast at this time of year, of all ages and social classes. SyanL people are unique about their vacations. A year ago, President Delonge promoted a vacation program where they were granted a generous bonus for vacations, only exchangeable for transportation and lodging, that bonus would have to be paid with discounts of thirty percent on their salaries, obviously with a high rate of interest. Delonge knows very well that the citizens of SyanL like to live well and enjoy themselves, even if it means suffering during the rest of the year.

Whiskey production at SyanL has dropped dramatically and that is why Daniel Delonge takes those steps. He is aware that it is the whiskey that his government must invest in and the resources must come from the people themselves.

Our nation is fickle, with inhabitants who have a weakness for wealth and perhaps the six of us carry that trait with intensity. In addition, SyanL is known for having inhabitants of general beauty, big eyes, a different brown each or an intense blue, a delineated mouth and a face that gives the impression of being always smiling. We are not perfect, but in other nations it is said that we get close enough, no matter the weight, height, or personality, in SyanL there is beauty. That is precisely the reason why it is so annoying for the inhabitants of my nation, not to be able to have the desired luxuries, that is how life in SyanL has been for a long time. The opposite of Toot's people. In Lola's nation, everyone works at forced marches and doesn't stop to wait. Toot's labor system is applauded and admired by many other nations; They only have one day off and this is optional, there are those who do not take it, their whiskey industry, for example. Countries like KanL, TyaL, Lonn are the hardest workers, but even they show admiration for Toot in that matter of productivity.

In SyanL this is not the case, President Daniel Delonge likes to give constant speeches about how important rest is, so that citizens can be able to give one hundred percent, he also emphasizes that despite the fact that our whiskey industry has two days of rest a week, it is enough for us to remain as the favorite inf the whole world, in terms of quality of the drink. And he is right. but even they show admiration for Toot in that regard.

However, recently the demonstrations and marches show that the people from SyanL do not want to be seen as a beautiful package, with nothing inside, they are people who suffer and Delonge seeks to remove that suffering, but he doesn't know how to do it, I doubt very much that killing Lola Teheran is the solution. I love my country, I venerate it and I have killed those who should be dead, those who beat it the most. But SyanL carries a natural disorder, in each one of us.

"I don't understand why we have to stay at the hotel for two days," Silfide murmurs next to me.

"Because we're not on vacation girl," Drider answers, rolling his eyes.

"I wasn't telling you," she says, he ignores her, as if the only thing that matters is what he said and continues.

"There is always the possibility that someone will discover us."

And as if Drider himself had called him, a guy in his early twenties, he approaches us. The first thing that strikes me is his silky light brown hair, as if he had spent hours in the beauty parlor and was on his way to a catwalk in Kaoy. He has bright eyes, the kind of eyes that hide a mischief of life. His smile is discreet, for a moment my gaze collides with his. The pleasant vision is clouded when my mind returns to that brutal morning at the airport, when we were caught.

He stops in front of us and our six Nexus begin to ring at the same time, I rush to take mine and it seems that it is enough, because they stop ringing when I answer.

"Yes?" I say.

"Corina? I would have preferred Jimmy to answer, but anyway. He is Joshua Castillo L." I look at him, and he raises an eyebrow, as if he knows that Reneé has just mentioned his name to me" from now on he will be with you guys all the time, ask no more, the only thing you need to know about him is that he is an expert in everything that you *say* you are," she emphasizes "being: weapons, explosives, etc. Joshua speaks seven languages, which you are fluent in and he has contacts at Toot. He is completely trusted by me and was appointed directly by President Delonge. That's all," and hangs up.

"No, Reneé, wait," I say, even knowing that the only answer is silence.

"Joshua" he says, offering me his hand, he looks at me and then at the others, "are we going now?"

"It's the first decision that I applaud that bitch!", says Silfide, throwing her luggage on the bed.

"He's nice, nothing to write home about," says Ondina.

"You're crazy to finish, the guy is beautiful," Silfide looks at her and Ondina looks down.

"I suppose he is very handsome," I finally say.

"Will affective relationships with him be allowed?" Silfide checks her makeup in front of the full-length mirror between her bed and mine.

"The guys weren't very happy when Joshua joined us," I say, and it's true. When we got to the hotel, Joshua said that he had to share a room with Estirge and during the drive to the place, Drider, Satiro and Estirge himself had a similar answer for each question that Joshua asked them.

"Did you travel a lot to the coast?" He had asked Satiro. Shrug.

"I like your watch, where did you buy it?", To Drider. Shrug.

"I once read a novel about mythology, it's interesting, I understand you like books" Estirge. Shrug.

And even so, those three gestures, Joshua didn't seem to care, he kept smiling, looking out the window.

"I like that it seems like he's about to laugh," I say suddenly, back in the room.

"Yes, yes, it's true" interrupts Ondina, "that's true, he has a beautiful smile."

"Didn't you just said that he was nothing to write home about?," laughs Silfide. Ondina rolls her eyes.

"Let's see, it is clear that he is handsome," she says, "I'm not blind either."

"That's not what you said a little while ago," Silfide insists.

"I'm not going to argue with you."

"Me neither, it just seems that sometimes you don't have your own opinion," she says, Ondina looks at her and then at me, confused.

"What?" she insists.

"Please, if Gorgona doesn't say she likes Joshua's smile, you wouldn't have said it either" explains Silfide.

Ondina looks at me insistently, I don't know what to say because it's true, so I look away.

"Do you also believe that?" she asks me. Fortunately, at that moment there is a knock on the door. I take the opportunity and stop to open.

"Shall I interrupt?" Is precisely the bone of contention, Joshua.

"Of course not!", Silfide walks up to him and pushes Ondina on his way, "come in, come in!"

"Thanks ... uh, Silfide right?

"Yes" she says, "or Dulce, as you like," she looks at him, playing with her own hair, but he remains undeterred.

"I hope I have not interrupted, say those who know that if you interrupt a female conversation, you will probably be the next topic," he says, his confidence seems to fill every room he steps on, the same effect that occurs when it comes to a writer young man or a gangster with elegance. Few produce such a thing, but Joshua with his light hair and laughing eyes does it.

"Then don't go!", laughs Silfide, touching his arm, "because we can eat you…" she laughs, "with words, once you leave the room!" warns my friend, Joshua laughs too. Ondina looks at me, we know that it is the way of being of Silfide, it always has been like that, she likes to attract the attention of men especially, with laughter, with looks, with shouts, with gestures, with poses. That's how she is, but in any case, Ondina's gaze pretends to be scandalized, as if she barely knew her.

"The truth is, I need to talk to you for a moment." Joshua turns to me. Ondina's eyebrows make an even more pronounced arch.

"Me?"

"Her?" Silfide lets go of his arm.

"Well, I'm actually taking turns talking to the six of you, getting to know your abilities, skills, stories, but" he clears his throat, "...the boys don't seem very open at the moment, I hope you do" he smiles at me. Now I am the one who clears my throat, I prepare my voice and I don't know where the urge to give such a ridiculous and constructed answer comes from.

"I can help you with pleasure," I say and I regret it instantly, I look like a pharmaceutical saleswoman, but Joshua smiles and his mischievous eyes get small. He points to the door and I follow.

Ondina and Sílfide may have argued previously, telling each other certain truths, but I'm sure that as soon as we close the door, they will start talking about us.

Joshua insisted that we stop by the hotel bar to order something. Deep down it gave me relief, but on the outside I told him that maybe talking under the influence of alcohol was not the best thing in itself. When the whiskey from the coast touches my lips, the first thing I think is about how uninteresting it tastes; Compared to SyanL, it tastes like heavy water.

The whiskey produced in SyanL is strong and you feel that its flavor explores every hole in your mouth, combining with your saliva to give the flavor that you like best: wood, seed, flower. Toot's whiskey will never outgrow us, least of all La Costa's.

"Where did you grow up?" Joshua tells me, I can see his disappointment when taking the first drink, he must be thinking the same thing as me.

"In Sy4, I have seen everything there, from the flood of 245 to the commercial depression in all sectors."

"That was hard, in Sy23 they showed the reports about it for more than a week," he says.

"Sy23 will never experience a depression like this, you have resources in everything, not only in the production of whiskey."

"Right," Joshua shrugs his shoulders, "but it is the whiskey that moves SyanL, so we must adapt," he takes a drink and finishes his glass, I'm still halfway there.

Silence takes over the environment for a few seconds, but it does not cause me discomfort, in fact I feel very good, perhaps it is the effect of the drink, a native of SyanL must find comfort in this amber liquid, we carry it in our blood. Maybe that's what we have in our veins: *whiskey*. And whiskey instead of blood itself, should be more beautiful to see if it spills.

"Do you have family?" Joshua glances at me, bites the stirring stick on his glass.

"I don't know where they are," I reply, avoiding the subject. This time I am the one who finishes the liquid without further ado.

"Oh I see. I'm sorry," he says.

"I thought Reneé and Delonge had given you a report on us," I observe.

"That's right, all the files are on my Nexus, but I prefer human contact, it always indicates more a look or an expression than something written in a profile."

"Shall we go back to the bar to ger another of this?" I show him my empty glass. Joshua nods, his smile has turned empathetic now.

"Is that why you are not scared? Because of the fact of not knowing anything about your family?", He asks suddenly. With these kinds of questions, I need another glass right now.

"No, it's not that."

"So? You have been killing very dangerous people for years and right now you are heading on an almost impossible mission."

"I remind you that you are going to the same mission," I point at him, and he laughs, contrasts with what he is about to say.

"Yes, I know, but I *am* scared."

"Me too," I answer, he blurted out. Joshua looks at me incredulously, like the father who discovers his daughter in the lie. We arrive at the bar and silently wait for our glass to be refilled. Anyway, this whiskey looks more like tap water.

"But you didn't feel like that before, right?"

"No" I answer still being honest.

"Why do you ask", I don't know if it's his tone of voice or his interest in my story, but I'm telling him something that I've never told anyone before.

"My family had always been strongly Catholic" I start, "when I came to the world, my parents took me to the church of *Santa Nicolasa,* which is located in the center of Sy4, where some paintings are currently exhibited. My parents told me once that they had brought me to the altar of that church and murmured: "She is yours, my lord, she will always be yours before being ours, so please, take care of her" and that's how it has been. It is not a memory of mine, but that is how they told me it happened. These were the last days of Catholicism, before temples became museum," He looks at me analytically.

"Knowing that God cares for you because your parents took you to him at birth" he murmurs.

"That in the situation that you believe in God."

"Sometimes I do" he explains, "sometimes I don't," his smile appears again, "but right now I have to say yes" his laugh comes out fresh and honest, "you know, just in case."

Joshua says it while looking to the horizon. The sea is distinguished from this point. I feel a fierce desire to jump in and swim to the end, even though it doesn't exist. It is strange that the sea and the desert share that immensity. And even with all its beauty, it is strange that I will always prefer the desert, because Sy4 is mainly that.

SyanL is mostly desert, especially the south and that's how I like it. Joshua and I returned to the rooms, our glasses no longer have any trace of the whiskey that in the end does not resemble SyanL's, but it made us talk. At least to me, Joshua was just asking.

CHAPTER

23

You could say that today is our last day of tranquility. Tomorrow we leave for Toot, separated, as Reneé indicated. It is three in the afternoon and we are sitting in one of the hotel restaurants, eating and waiting for drinks.

"We could do something tonight," I suggest, I've thought about it all day, I know what it is and I don't want to say it, but Drider examines me with his hard eyes and says it.

"Like a goodbye thing?"

"What's with the negativity?", Exclaims Silfide, splitting her salmon "it would rather be a…" she takes the pink bite of the fish in and continues, with her mouth full "... a celebration prior to the success we will have," she corrects. Joshua laughs and I catch a glimpse of Satiro looking at him like he's looking at a child trying to get their parents' attention by jumping and screaming.

"It's a good idea," Ondina says very seriously, she is still a little mad at Silfide for having told her that she has no opinion of her own.

"Satiro and Ondina have to leave tomorrow on the seven o'clock train," says Estirge. I realize that I haven't

145

talked to him lately, and now what he says is for the group, not for me.

"Well, yes," I answer looking at him directly, "but it's not like they are going to drive the train", Estirge looks at me, I know he has nothing to refute, I hold his brown and warm gaze. It is unique and exudes security, but I am afraid, I am always afraid of losing it.

"It doesn't matter," he finishes, it gives the impression that he is no longer talking about the train.

"We could go to the bar for a while and that's it," Satiro suggests, wiping his lips with a small white napkin. Sometimes his innate neatness only serves to remind me how messy I can be, I look at my already empty plate, full of little paper balls, of a torn napkin.

"The whiskey here," Drider mutters, "is disgusting, by the way, I prefer to drink water from all the bathrooms together," he complains, but with that comment I realize that he has accepted, even though he mentioned it as a farewell.

The worst thing is that he is right, it may be a farewell and that is why we must do it. I read it on everyone's faces, even Joshua's.

"Well, I'll pass" Estirge gets up, "have fun" he says before putting down his napkin and leaving.

I am the one who comes out after him and it is Satiro who comes out after me and takes my arm.

"What are you doing, Gorgona?" He says, he has wavy locks of hair on his forehead.

"What does it look like? I'm going to see what happens with Estirge, thanks" I try to let go, he does not leave my arm and although he does not press me, people could suspect or seeing something strange in us, but in someway, Satiro does it so it seems like a caress in the eyes of the rest of the diners.

"Well, are you stupid? It is obvious that he must be angry about something, let him to cool off"

"Jair," I take his real name, "you don't have to tell me what to do and what not to do, so please let me go, we are making a scene", with my eyes I point to the rest of the restaurant, he laughs, nobody is watching us, "Well, okay there's no scene, but I'm going to talk to him, if you don't let me go now, I'll do it later or later, or later or late-" Satiro finally lets go.

"Don't spoil the mission Corina, please", he warns me, he uses my real name in a kind of revenge then he goes back to the table.

I catch up with Estirge just before he opens the door to his room.

"Estirge," I say, he turns with all the naturalness of the world; I expected an angry face, fed up, annoyed, full of anger, perhaps jealousy. He joins his lips to form a thin line, a common gesture on his face, however, he doesn't say a word, "what's wrong? "I insist, standing in front of him.

"About what?" He answers, I see that his eyes are irritated and for a stupid moment I think he has been crying for me. But he doesn't cry, he never has.

"Why did you leave the restaurant like that?"

"How?" He continues with his neutral expression, and the worst: he continues to put the electronic key in the door indicating that he has no intention of talking to me.

"So ... sudden," I feel ridiculous with every word I say.

"I want to take a nap," he shrugs, "that's it."

"And what about tonight plan?" I insist, if I'm already here maybe the best thing is to get to the bottom of the matter. I'm not going to embark on a near-suicidal mission without being okay with him.

"What about it?" He asks, I think I see a hint of doubt in his eyes, as if he really doesn't know what I mean, and the truth is… what do I mean?

"We will all go to the bar, except you," I tell him and at the same time I realize that compared to what awaits us soon, drinking tonight sounds absurd.

"I have no intention of going to any bar and I think that neither should you."

"Why not?" I question insistently, he has his hand holding the door, he doesn't even seem eager to invite me in and I'm still here, almost pleading. What a bit of a loser I am.

"You risk being seen, identified or getting drunk and doing something stupid."

"We have been working on this for years and that includes you, where do you get the idea that we would do something as stupid as get drunk and throw everything away?", I claim. His gesture transforms from neutral to jaded in a second.

"Look Corina, this is my point of view, do you understand? It's up to you and the others if you want to risk your skin for a few fucking drinks", he says, looking at me and then I don't know what to say to him. I realize it's impossible to agree, "besides, I have to talk to Reneé about some details of the plan."

"Good," I murmur, feeling a twinge of jealousy, before turning around and heading back to the restaurant where I know no one will ask me what happened.

CHAPTER

25

I like whiskey glasses because they are roomy. We have gone through a journey to be able to buy a bottle originally from SyanL and nothing compares to that whiskey. Toot has the money, the industry, the machinery, the image, the marketing and the Sales skill, but they do not have the talent of creation, their whiskey will never have the taste of wood, the cotton on the lips, the aroma of wet brick, the caress of glass before cutting, all those experiences that only SyanL whiskey gives.

Lola Tehran's corruption and international networks will never reach to ruin our distillate. Never. And I'm not the one saying it. I am hearing drunken coastal citizens say that the beauty of tall Toot bottles will never be enough to make you dizzy in love, as SyanL whiskey does, even if it is served in dull. plastic cups.

And I know it, I lived it, SyanL's most famous whiskey, *Joan Megghia,* tastes like everything: the smell of wet sand from the sea, green walnuts, ground and fermented corn, a pinch of sugar in keep, just a pinch. The *Tino Tawrr* whiskey, our second best, smells a bit of the marker that is prohibited to smell, of the new and hot plastic, of the cardboard stored for many years, of guitar strings, that's what our whiskey smells like, like an old dictionary, like porcelain from the finest.

Our third best whiskey, the *Jooly Rodz* hurts and hits hard, like when you are ignored or humiliated, pushing you aside. It hurts like the gesture of shame of yours, it hurts like the coffin, the hug at a funeral, like this, with that impact. It hurts like swallowing when you can't, it hurts like the first scolding of your life, and if you don't remember, SyanL whiskey makes you remember it.

Those from the south don't like it, they produce rum and it is the only thing that they like, they speak of whiskey with envy, with the fury that a frustrated girl speaks badly of her friend behind her back. But still with that, they speak a lot about our whiskey.

It is impossible to summarize all the sensations that this SyanL product can cause you, so I do not understand how Estirge chose not to experience them once more. Maybe one last.

"Is everything alright?", Silfide says to me when she catches me looking at the ice that looks like river stones in my glass. They are green in color and contrast with amber in an exquisite way.

"I don't know," I answer, "do you want the short version?"

"You know what they say: these are times of hurry."

"I think they are like that since I killed the first person on my list," I answer, not surprising that I don't feel a trace of guilt.

"What happened today, Gorgona?" Silfide looks at me and I don't know how she does it but she's also looking at the waiter with a smile from her most sensual catalog. When I see him he's already pouring whiskey and tonic inside her glass. Everyone has their style to drink it. My dad used to say that the best whiskey is dry, that he wanted that as his last drink. The best flavors were my mother's kisses and dry whiskey. Each citizen drinks it in their own way, perhaps the inhabitants of SyanL drink it with the left hand or with a tired or broken tongue.

"And so? What happened?" Silfide insists.

"I don't know what's wrong with Estirge lately."

"Gorgona, he's jealous," she says, taking a quick drink, "and Drider too, if we are strict, maybe Satiro is jealous too, they don't like Joshua," and so, as if that were the end point, Silfide gets up and I remain there at the bar, thinking, with the company that the inhabitants of SyanL are used to: a flat and short glass.

CHAPTER

26

I get off the plane and the cold wind from Toot penetrates my eyes, I don't know if it's a natural hostility from this place, but I feel them reddening. I walk into the airport and through the glass walls I see the tall and square buildings of this place, almost all of them are steel color, some earth tones stand out but most of them are gray. Toot is boring even at that. Among the constructions there are some spectacular banners very well aligned, announcing different brands of Whiskey, from here, of course.

I look at my Nexus, before leaving the airport, I must wait for the message from Reneé, with the address and name of the hotel, as well as my reservation information. I have two packages of documents with me: the false and the authentic. The first ones say that my name is Corina A. T and that I was born in LaGem twenty years ago, I am a medical student.

The real ones indicate that my name is Corina A. T, I am eighteen years old, born in SyanL, a member of a group of teens, *The Animalium*, who kill for money.

It is ten past eleven at night and I have not received the data, it is supposed that these should have arrived to my Nexus at eleven. I do not like this, I look around and there are no familiar faces, Estirge and Joshua would travel at the same time as me, if at all a few minutes apart, therefore they should already be around. Maybe Reneé decided to do this without me. I look at my Nexus over and over, run my fingers over the transparent touchscreen, and nothing. I cannot go to any hotel, I must not even move from here. Why am I always the one left alone? The one they leave out? This can't be right in any way. Where are they? I feel that people look at me with a certain suspicion, that I look so foreign, and everyone knows who I am.

I take a few steps and collide with a tall, bearded man.

"Sorry" I say, and I keep walking through the airport, I look at my Nexus and nothing, I hold my suitcase tightly. No, it is better to go to the exit door, at least I must be near it. I don't know why I'm holding my luggage so tightly.

"It's her!... Miss?", I know it's me who is being called, I don't see that they point at me, but I know they mean me.

"Miss?!. Excuse me?", I walk quickly towards the exit, some faces turn to see me, to every step the knot in my stomach grows "Excuse me?!, stop her!", I manage to listen, I throw the suitcase on the ground and with the bag of documents firmly held in my hands I cross the exit door, I run with all the power that my legs give me, there are many people outside and that complicates things for them, for those that are after me, I keep running until I reach a dark corner in the street, my agitated breathing is heard as if it had a personal and strong echo. From here I see the commotion:

a tall guard with big teeth points towards where I am, but also he doubt about the opposite street, two groups of four guards run in both directions; If I move they will see me, there is no doubt, But if I wait in this darkness maybe I can go unnoticed My hands are cold despite the heat that adrenaline produces, I tremble no matter the sweat that runs down my face, I hear the footsteps of the guards and although I want to close my eyes, I know that I should not. I am grateful for not having done it because then something happens that I will remember as one of the most relieving moments in my life: the blue lights of a car that is meters away come to where I am, it accelerates and pulls to the side of where I am hiding, the door opens and Joshua from inside yells at me.

"Gorgona, come up! Quick!" and I do it, I come out of my hiding place, out of the corner of my eye I can see that there are no longer just four guards, but about twenty who are heading to where I was. I get into the car and we start at full speed, my breathing continues so agitated that I am not able to ask anything, Joshua and Estirge look at me and I cannot even identify their expressions, even so it is Joshua who is speaking.

"Something went wrong."

"Everything!", Estirge kicks the closet while screaming. The room in this hotel is semi-lit, I look at them, they both have a very different way of expressing concern.

Joshua is sitting on the dirty, rough bed next to me. His hand holds his face, he looks down at the floor, I don't know what he is so carefully observing. Estirge mutters to himself, pacing back and forth across the room. I feel a heavy anxiety in my stomach, my head buzzes, and my eyes ... I don't know, I don't know where to look, where to direct them, I could travel the whole room and the answer will not be there. I'm startled by the vibration coming from Joshua's Nexus. Lately this anguish lasts longer, that moment before what will be bad news, is painful and shakes even worse than the news itself. It is the feeling that has been with me in recent weeks. The same feeling I experienced when my family disappeared.

"Joshua", he responds by pressing a button on his Nexus, Estirge looks at him, I don't dare to do it, I'm scared that his expression could indicate the worst, I bite the nail of my little finger and now I'm the one who examines the ground. I would like to cover my ears but I don't want to be so ridiculous either, so I have no choice but to listen to what

Joshua answers, "Yes, well, that's right, there is no other way," he hangs up and I finally dare to look at him.

"And?" Estirge interrogates him, outside cats are heard in the middle of the night. This hotel belongs to Joshua, the land was given to him by a relative who lives in Toot, or that's what he explained. Nobody uses it as such, sometimes some of the very few bums in this city come in. Joshua mentioned that it is sometimes a haven for stolen Nexus dealers. The room smells of old food and cigarettes.

I look at Joshua but his narrowed eyes don't tell me anything, if I knew him better I would know what those lips mean, turning almost invisible, like a horizon obscured by the sun. I feel a dry fear inside me.

"No information has been spread. Yet," he says, "they don't know we're here, they don't know about *us*, but they do have the certainty that you are," their eyes pierce me, cold. Estirge also looks at me and speaks harshly:

"Did you talk to someone?" He says and I can't believe that the one who has been my accomplice for years is asking me that. However, that is only the beginning. Estirge takes me by the shoulders and makes me get out of bed, he holds me too tightly and you can see that he tries not to raise his voice, "Gorgona?"

"No! But what are you saying!"

"Who?" he insists "Who the hell did you talk to? When?"

"Let go of me!" I finally push him away, taking his hands off me. I look at him with hatred, more for doubting me than for treating me so rudely. My eyes go to Joshua, asking for his support, but he checks his Nexus and has no idea of the tension between me and Estirge. I close my eyes and breathe as deeply as I can, my lungs still feel empty.

"I didn't say anything" I try to explain, "I didn't talk to anyone either, it's clear that someone betrayed us, or that there is a flaw in the plan, we let go of some detail."

"The plan was perfect," Joshua speaks at last, he addresses us both, "we detailed it and studied it, we had everything outlined, without blemishes and-"

"Have we?" interrupts Estirge with his now usual very suspicious tone "as far as I know, you joined suddenly and well" he insists sarcastically "the truth is that we don't know you well, you arrived at the last minute," now the icy look that a few moments ago pierced me is on Joshua.

"Don't forget that I joined on Delonge's orders, not for the pleasure," he answers with a serenity that makes his sarcasm more refined "to accompany you" he ends. Estirge looks at him with helplessness, he knows that there is no claim that is worth it, that if Joshua is there it is because the president of SyanL gave the order.

"What am I going to do?" I say suddenly, making them return to reality where I am at risk. Where my current situation is the only thing that matters to me for now.

"We have to wait for instructions."

"From whom?" I look at Joshua as if it were his fault. "From Reneé?, From the person who doesn't give a shit about what happens to me?"

"Whatever happens to us," Estirge corrects. I am bothered by his inclusion, anyone with three fingers of a forehead could see the preference that Reneé always showed over him. Joshua's Nexus vibrates again, there are the fucking instructions.

"Joshua," he says, his impassive gaze, I do not want anything more at this moment than knowing what is behind those malt whiskey-colored eyes "very well" he hangs up and something weighs in his gaze, after all he is not so expressionless.

"You will have to stay here, the mission will be suspended for a couple of days at most, in which you will wait locked up. In any case, the Ramón de Barbé Gala will be until Thursday."

"What? What are you saying?" My head tingles "NO! I can't stay here; I'm not going to stay here!"

"You don't have a choice" he insists, he doesn't even look at me "for food and water don't worry, I'll take care of everything."

"No!" I interrupt, "Estirge, I can't stay here!, Do something!" I exclaim, Joshua types in his Nexus and an image is projected, it is me at the airport, the video is repeated over and over again, you can see how I leave and go into the dark street.

"Is it the network?" Asks Estirge.

"No, it's a file from the Toot Nation Security Guard," Joshua explains, the video stops and large and clear letters appear above it:

ALLEGED INTRUDER INTO THE SOVEREIGN NATION OF TOOT.

Corina TA

Nation of SyanL

Location unknown

Reasons for internment using a fake identity in the Toot nation: Unknown.

Companies: None detected so far.

I look at the projection, my eyes are about to fill with tears, I dig my nails into the palm of my hand avoiding crying, distracting myself with physical pain.

"They are not sure that it is you, as you can see, but if you expose yourself immediately, they will be and the rest of us will be in the eye of the hurricane."

"Joshua, I can't, I just can't stay here locked up like a fucking lion until Reneé considers it to be ..."

"It has nothing to do with Reneé!" Exclaims Estirge, desperate. I get the impression that he is hiding something from me.

"And how do you know?" I need to convince them not to leave me here.

"Don't be stupid," he tells me and it becomes clearer that I am unable to recognize him, to adapt to his attitude in recent days. We used to be different, cold blood never manifests between us. It hurts me to know that apparently everything has changed, this topic hurts because I know it is endless.

"I need you to be aware of your Nexus all the time," indicates Joshua, "we could come back for you tomorrow or tonight, I don't know yet, you should sleep the four hours strictly necessary and at the slightest threat, flee."

"Only if there were any," Estirge clarifies with his paternalistic tone. The resignation that invades me is like that of a medical diagnosis without turning back. The worst of my fears.

The room is still dark and, in these shadows, I see them go. I watch them walk away and close the door, their shadow contrasts almost like a sunrise with the bluish light that comes from the street. I am not saying goodbye.

It is not the confinement; it is the fear that it causes me. It smells of wet brick, I feel like this scent will never go away and it could still be the last thing I smelled in my life. I can't go out, I can't look for them, I don't know if I'd be exposing them, I have no idea the name of their hotel.

As if they were hammering me in the head, I hear the sound of footsteps climbing rapidly. Not only that, but a murmur of vehicles also peeks out the window even in the distance.

"Gorgona," Silfide's voice behind the door lifts me up as if an electric shock ran through the entire floor of this old hotel. I open the door and she gets in, and goes to the window, leaves a package on the floor, I feel that rush that always emanates from her.

"Change your clothes" she pulls out a 710 goldgun and stands near the window "come on, we don't have much time! Change!" she repeats, I open the package and find a black anti-metal lycra suit like the one she is wearing. I dress as fast as I can, the blue boots are my exact size. Inside the package there is also a goldgun 900, I handle them better than the 710.

"Let's go," she says, takes a last look at the street and we go out the door of the room. We went down the stairs quickly, but we did not go to the main entrance. Silfide guides me down a narrow brick hallway, it's damp and the scent penetrates my nose even further. At the end there is a rusty door and much narrower than the corridor, when crossing it, Sílfide makes her way towards the street, and I follow her.

The noise of cars and high-pitched sirens, with a constant chirping, characteristic of Toot's alarms, is heard closer and closer.

We go towards a gray vehicle with dark windows and when I take a quick glance, I see that the street is full of many more, all the same. It is a passenger car but a little bigger, when I get in, they are all there. Fear, far from dispersing when seeing them, grows. Being all together, I am struck by the assurance that we could die very soon. We risk everything and the possibility that we will lose is enormous.

For more than three hours, Joshua drives avoiding the guards. Drider hasn't stopped staring at his Nexus for a single moment. I have not wanted to give them the pleasure of asking where we are going or what the new plan is, I do not want to feel left out again. Also, they all look very focused, worried, or maybe both. When I'm about to give up and ask, Joshua stops in front of another hotel even more ramshackle than the last.

"Here it is," he says. The car's locks are deactivated, and the doors open.

I can barely make out the facade, it was once white but now is dirty, full of soot and graffiti with Toot's symbols and in its colors, blue and black, faded and without strength.

We follow Joshua, he opens the door with an old metal key, the place is very old and those keys have not been used in Toot or SyanL for more than seventy years.

"Platinum level?" Silfide's voice echoes inside that place, which looks even worse inside: dirt, rubble, and I'm sure there is a trail of blood on the wall to my right.

"What did you expect?" Satiro replies "we are hiding, this isn't the moment to stand out, that will be later, when we return as heroes," he completes with his characteristic security. He can speaks for himself, I do not seek to transcend, quite the opposite.

"It is nine at night, we will sleep here today and at seven in the morning we will change headquarters. Ramon rescheduled his Gala for the day after tomorrow night, because of Alex Zendejas, who for some reason, could not attend in the date that was scheduled"

"Him? Who?" I ask and I regret it instantly, I know who Joshua is referring to even before Estirge clarifies it for me. But I feel so confused by everything, that I don't what I'm saying.

"Ramón de Barbé."

"The mission begins tomorrow in the new headquarters," Ondina says, the reproach in her voice is evident, "we have already talked about it."

"And how could I know? I was secluded all day yesterday, in case you haven't noticed," I say. She narrows her eyes, I see that the mermaid that is almost identical to my viper shines on her neck, I put my hand to my chest and my anger grows, it irritates me as she copies everything almost cheekily, including my symbol, and I continue:

"¿Did you notice it? Did you notice my absence or were you too busy trying to be caught as well?" I say, I know that maybe I've gone overboard, but I hate that tendency of hers to explain things, plans, events, memories that for a reason happened when I wasn't there, and I hate even more the fact that she does it like having a complicity with Estirge.

"Right in one thing," she answers, apparently none of us is going to stay in silence "I was *busy*, investigating data on the network, like all of us," she opens her arms to support her words, encompassing the others, "to know how the hell the system of Toot's security found out that you were here, what is this about? Is that why you wanted to escape as Drider made that suggestion? Did you give us away and want your skin safe?" His face pales, causing acne on his forehead stick out more.

"Shut up, Ondina" Silfide intervenes.

"Why don't you worry about your own things? I don't know, flirt with Sátiro or complain about the place, something that suits your way of being," she answers. I do not understand where she wants to go with her words, but he lights the fuse of Silfide.

"I assure you that if Gorgona had betrayed us, you would be there, doing the same thing, always in her shadow, always imitating her!" Laughs Silfide laughing out loud. Satiro looks at her in surprise, even though he knows her well.

"Enough of childishness," Drider's voice has always been the most powerful, "save the stupidity for when we return to SyanL" he suggests. Inside of me I know that we are not going to return and if so, it will be to never see each other again.

Ondina looks at him with hatred and goes to the edge of the room, where there are some old cardboard. She sits down and takes out her Nexus, forgetting about us.

We each do it eventually. Silfide sits on the moldy wooden staircase, it hurts me that she doesn't come near me, that she doesn't ask me to sit with her, but I can make out her gaze and she's absorbed in the plan. If there is something Silfide has, it is that she reviews things over and over again. Before, whenever Drider proposed or designed a strategy, it has always been Silfide who studied it the most.

Satiro and Estirge find two chairs and exchange opinions aided by the lights of their Nexus. Joshua paces the room, eventually he goes upstairs, speaking on his Nexus, probably with Reneé. The network of our devices has been protected thanks to Drider. I don't understand how my location was discovered. I look at Drider, he's sitting on the floor next to a window with thick, smoked glass. I observe him carefully, his black hair, his wicked gray eyes, full of all his history, I have seen those eyes enjoy when he hits someone mercilessly, I have seen those thin lips smile because of the nasty people blood spilled dozens of times. While I think about it, I am walking towards him and without thinking I put my hand in my pocket, I take out the gun and point it directly at him.

"Why didn't you protect my Nexus from Toot's net?" I demand without lowering the weapon. I know everyone sees me, Satiro and Estirge stand up. Sílfide and Ondina do the same, Joshua is still upstairs, "Why?" Drider's eyes, full of sadness surprise me like few things have done before.

CHAPTER

30

"What's going on?", Joshua runs down, he perceives the tension, that must be his greatest quality.

"Drider did not protect my Nexus, that's why they located me," I explain without lowering the weapon, the momentary sweetness in the gray eyes disappears and without making any attempt to defend himself, he responds.

"Your Nexus was the first one that I gave myself to the task of protecting" now his expression is hard, "I did the same with each one," he says resolutely. I'd like to put down my goldgun, but I can't, it must be him! It has to be him! Why do I feel this? Where does this insistence to accuse my childhood friend come from?

"Put your weapon away, Gorgona, Drider is telling the truth," Joshua explains, "the software is on my own Nexus and they are all synchronized," he says. It's so simple and I feel ridiculous, so much so that I still can't put this shit away.

Finally the mocking face of Ondina makes me want to be the big person in the room and I put the gun down.

"Sorry," I whisper, barely in a sigh.

Drider stands up, I see him without blinking, his dark hair, his big eyes, his thin mouth, the newspaper on which he was sitting makes a lot of noise, that noise is the background of the image that will remain etched in my head forever: he approaches in a hurry, as if fleeing and kisses me.

I don't know how much time passes, or what my head sums up but I don't like it. Four, five seconds. When the feeling of icy surprise passes, I weakly push him, openly showing my confusion toward his kiss, and run up the stairs.

The first thing I notice is that the carpet on the second floor is eaten away as if it had suffered burns, it is the only thing I see because it is difficult for me to even look up, I go into the first room in front of me and close the door. I don't want to hear what they're saying downstairs, I don't even know if they're saying anything, but I cover my ears with both hands and slowly flop onto the wet, dirty floor of what was once an elegant piece, but which at this moment smells of mold and earth.

If a few moments ago I pointed to him ready to kill him if he was the traitor, now I feel the same desire for him to leave and disappear. Not a minute goes by when I hear the door to the room open. Whoever enters, I feel him lean next to me with the elegance and silence of an expert. He says nothing, but in the stillness I can even feel his breathing. I take my hands off my ears and slowly turn my head. Satiro' straight-nosed profile and barely protruding lips are beside me, he is lying on his back with his eyes open.

"In these instances," he says, "I think I'd even give up the life of one of you for a glass of Joan Megghia on the rocks," he says, referring to the best whiskey from SyanL. The comment makes me smile, due to the familiarity of that name, and at the same time it scares me to know that it is not such a bad idea.

"Do you think that with even a sip, everything would improve?" I ask him, my voice is even weaker than his.

"Maybe yes, whiskey… *water of life*," he laughs "it is ironic that this being its meaning, we have to die for it."

"Maybe it takes more than one sip."

"If you like strong emotions," he looks at me and smiles, "then I suppose so."

Neither of us says anything for a moment. I feel that there is something that I do not know, that in my absences, that before meeting Delonge and when I arrived at Toot, things have happened that nobody wants to tell me, but I have no way of finding out.

"What is a strong emotion?" I finally whisper.

"Birth is quite strong," he answers without taking his eyes off the ceiling, the place where once there was perhaps a crystalline lamp.

"And the opposite?"

"Die? Is much stronger" he explains, "because at birth you are not aware that you are being born," sighs, "and when you die, you are aware, especially with our lifestyle," he says and he does it with such freshness that that cold of his words It gives me the kind of night shudder that is only felt in abandoned cemeteries or convents. Satiro sighs longingly again.

"*Water of life,* or in the end, water of death, is still part of us."

"Even if it wasn't on the rocks, I would accept it," he says, he always drinks it like that, otherwise it bores him, "I would accept it anyway, even with that disgusting lime flavor that Silfide likes so much," I smile, it's true, my friend, unlike him, prefers it with that citrus taste.

"Satiro?" I begin, he raises his eyebrows, as if giving me the word. "Could it be that we have given the liquor a romance that it does not have, so that way we don't feel bad when drinking it?"

"I guess so. It doesn't really taste good, to be honest," hearing him say those words hits me in the gland of disappointment. SyanL is that, SyanL is whiskey, SyanL's work translates to whiskey and Satiro is absolutely right: alcohol does not taste good.

"What will happen when the world finds out?" I ask, although we may not live long enough to see how the planet notices that this strong flavor is not so pleasant.

"Gorgona, the whole world knows it, they have known since thousands of years ago. We know it when we take the first drink, we do not drink it because of the taste on the tongue, we drink it because of the taste in the guts".

I go down the stairs with Satiro by my side, I can make out through the high windows that the moon hides behind wide clouds.

"Everything okay?" Joshua asks, his voice with a northern SyanL accent filling the entire room.

"Everything ok," Satiro explains, "except that we don't have a drop of whiskey to toast," he answers, I avoid looking at Drider, and although I am not sure, I know that he also avoids me.

"No? Are you sure?" Joshua smiles without losing that leadership that has characterized him since he arrived, even without giving a single order.

I look in the direction of Estirge, for some reason, I hope to see him upset, maybe because of the kiss, but no, from his coat bag he takes out a round, amber glass bottle, small, the size of a hand, the cap is shaped diamond, blue. *Joan Megghia*, says on the label. My eyes go from the bottle to Estirge's gaze, he smiles and looks at me too, something makes him happy, something makes him re-emerge those gestures that I thought he had forgotten. That smile kindles my soul. I don't know if it's the whiskey or if he feels like everyone else and he has given up.

It is four in the morning, today we will change headquarters. Even so, all I have in mind is what happened last night, everything, Drider's kiss, the toast we made and that could have been the last. My stomach is still pounding from excitement or nerves. I would like to go out and find a coffee shop but I don't know if I can do it and I also don't know where there might be a business open in Toot at this time in the morning.

My head goes over the scenes from the night before, I get up and I try to avoid making noise on the creaking wood. Through the window a small yellow moon can be seen, its edges so outlined that it looks like a marble about to fall on us.

"I like it better than the sun" Estirge's voice at my side startles me, "at least the moon can be seen directly without going blind".

I see *him*, his oval face, with his hair in eternal mess, is precisely illuminated by that moon of which he speaks. I don't know what to answer, I suddenly feel shy and I think I'll just say nonsense.

From the corner of my eye I see his silhouette. Outside, isolated sounds of cars can be heard, nearby there are whiskey distillers that work the night shift. They are in operation twenty-four hours a day and even this area there is the noise of work.

"What are you thinking" He asks, in a low voice, I look him in the eye and I'm scared that my answer might even bore him. It has been so recurring the last few days.

"What else?" I shrug my shoulders and I feel a start in my chest when I see him smile, he knows what I mean, this fear that assails me every day since that demonstration in which we ended up caught.

"Whatever has to happen will happen," he says, "whether we like it or not," he points out without stop looking at the moon.

"What scares you the most, Jimmy?" I ask him, using his real name, that name that almost no one uses, except than his father when he lived.

"Happiness, because I feel fragile," when he looks at me with the intense brown of his eyes, the moon continues to illuminate his face.

"And now? Are you happy?" I stutter.

"Happy ... and terrified," he says, his face is so close to mine. It feels like this was going to happen since the beginning of times, since both of us were nothing but dust around that same moon.

181

181

And it was as if everything around us began to fade, like when in a movie we are transported to a memory, to a beautiful memory, black and white, to a French and jazz memory. So was Estirge's closeness, his face so close, his eyes examining mine, not the rest of my face, just my eyes, his hands exploring my waist and his lips about to touch mine. While the unknown and cold Toot melted around us, like wax, in my head many moments lived by his side. Like that dinner, in a French restaurant, when we learned a year ago that six reporters had been murdered by SyanL's Federal Recruitment Commissioner, Jaime Crest. Killed in cold blood, naked and hanged in strategic places in Sy23, showing photos of their families over their bodies, stapled to their hands and feet. Jaime Crest was never blamed, but it was evident, months before those same reporters had exposed him for influence peddling and embezzlement in the Recruitment Monetary Fund.

"It's the most complicated," Satiro had said, drinking his double whiskey in one gulp. "Families!... The families of the reporters, they, the ones who remain! Those who survive!"

"What do you mean?" Silfide asked at the time, a little lost in her attitude, she had never been a family girl.

"I mean that they, the reporters, are already dead. Yes, it is painful, outrageous and Jaime Crest is going to pay for it," Satiro had said, looking at Ondina in a significant way, since she would be in charge of finishing him, "but they are no longer there, they no longer feel and although surely the moment was terrible, what they did to them, the anguish of not knowing ..." he had said, looking at me, as if doubting, probably thinking about how I did know nothing about my own family, "but hey, it's over, they are no longer here but their families are, they are the ones who have to live with that weight and with that pain. Jaime Crest lit a spark that will not end until it is consumed." He drank the rest of the whiskey, "that's pretty much the definition of *violence*"

At that moment, Satiro had raised a hand to call the waiter, I remember looking at my knee-length black dress, before getting up, brushing some invisible dust spots from my lap and going out for a breath.

I know Satiro hadn't said all that speech for me, but I couldn't help feeling hinted at and overwhelmed. My family, where were they? I didn't know, and that song played by Satiro hurt like a hot shackle on the face.

I remember how it was cold outside even when it was May. I couldn't help but think about what he had said, about those poor families, how the world had turned viciously for them, like a cold climate in a warm season.

Despite the heavy traffic in the center of SyanL, I felt that the street outside that restaurant was so narrow, that the cars were painted, that they had no edges or dimensions, I felt that that cold was not typical of that May, but from an icy December many years ago.

The French restaurant was fronted by tall, pink windows, through which I saw Estirge go to where I was, on the sidewalk of the street. His gray suit contrasted with the dark brown of his hair, which as always moved in the night breeze.

He went out whistling *La Vie en Rose*. I remember now in his eyes how that night he went through the whole melody before he started talking outside that restaurant.

"I started to think about what Satiro said, about families, I started to think about the people I love and who are not part of my family," he had said, with his hands in the pockets of his gray suit, looking at the same moon, "I have many choices to think about, but you came to my mind in the first place," his confusing gesture, but at the same time remarking something obvious, "I was surprised and perhaps I tried to evade, thinking of other people, until without realizing it I started to think mostly of you. There you are. Like when someone makes a gesture, or I read something about feelings, you know? , you immediately come to mind."

I remember the exact tone of voice and the gestures of Estirge when he told me all that, at a time when all I needed was fresh air and he gave me more than that, with a few simple words.

Today we are a few hours away from risking our lives, maybe I will never see myself in those eyes again and it scares me. I want to remember everything, everything, now that I have him in front of me, now, in this garbage dump of a place where we wait for the right time, here, surrounded by rubble, old newspapers and moldy walls, surrounded by colleagues just as fearful as we are.

"Jimmy," I tell him, savoring his name, the one he doesn't like to be used, the one that he doesn't let anyone uses, but me. "if we die ..."

"Nobody's going to die. You won't," he interrupts me, I open my mouth to continue the moving speech I was thinking of giving, but I don't say anything, I see him approach and kiss me with such a deep intensity that it seems to prove the opposite of what he just said: it seems that we are seconds away of leaving the earth forever and that this is his farewell, I hug him and I don't want to let go, I contrast him with Drider's kiss and there is no minimum level of comparison between the two. Jimmy is everything, it's the sounds he makes when he kisses me and the warmth of his face, it's the familiar scent that his skin gives off so close to me.

It still tastes like whiskey, ice and I know that from then on, if I survive, no drink is going to taste the same, they will all be terrible compared to this combination. I don't know how long it lasts, there are no units of time that can measure this moment that marks a complete continent in my life. But it is the sound of footsteps creaking on the stairs that makes us part. When I move away from his lips I feel dizzy, but I don't know if it's because I stopped kissing him or because I did it in the first place.

I turn around and I see that Ondina is already at the foot of the stairs and sees us, her face shows no surprise, in a way, there is a resignation in her eyes, which she knows eternal. The others are still coming down, their footsteps are light but the place is so old that the wood creaks. It is Joshua who speaks.

"It's time," he says.

"It's still early morning" I answer, looking at my Nexus, my mouth feels sore from the kiss. Joshua raises an eyebrow and makes a half smile before answering.

"There is a slight change of plans."

CHAPTER

35

The contrast is almost absurd. A few hours ago we were in the worst sty in Toot and now we are in the lobby of Suits & Royal Inc., the most exclusive hotel in this nation. For some reason, its minimalist structures, its white walls, immaculate floors and its employees, are all attractive, from the bellman who greets us at the door, with his light and wavy hair, contrasting with his black eyes, to the receptionist who attends us, a redhead, with cinnamon-colored skin, green eyes and lips like a small rosebud. This environment makes me more uncomfortable than the dump we were in before, but I can't guess why.

We go in our disguise as impertinent and annoying heirs, we now are young people way busy thinking about the party, the alcohol, and the conquests, or at least that is the impression we want to give.

At the reception there are two people, we go to the redhead with green eyes who welcomes us with a smile. It's Joshua who's running the record. The receptionist seems delighted with him, even making a comment about the nice things he can visit in Toot. I don't know how. Toot can be productive, with a lot of progress, work and order, but it is not beautiful. Joshua however, pretends to be delighted with the information the girl tells him. I'm not interested in their flirtation.

However, the other receptionist, the short-haired blonde, is not having such a good time: a young woman looks at her with annoyance and complains. The client is a broad girl, with heavy arms and a deep voice, her gesture perfectly suits her unhappy attitude.

"I don't get it! I just can't understand what I'm doing here! Arguing with a rude employee about whether I have the reservation!"

"Miss, as I indicated, there is no registration and this needs to be done at least two hours in advance, if you like to wait no more than ten minutes, we will make an exception and register you," the blonde behind the reception tries not to lose temper.

"This is absurd! Do you know who I am?" The obese young woman points to herself while with her other hand she takes out a card from her shiny handbag.

"Please don't bother miss, all our guests deserve an excellent treatment, understanding and respect, that's why I insist on asking if you want me to do the registration," the receptionist does her best to keep smiling. She must be very well trained for these situations because the other does not give her arm to twist.

"I am Dora Tarín De Barbé, niece of the President of the Toot Communications Network, Ramón de Barbé,", she says. The mention of the name makes the seven of us look at each other on alert, trying to be as discreet as possible.

This is it: she is the cause of the *slight change of plans.*

"I traveled thousands of kilometers from Kaoy, I left my fashion school, I traveled on a plane that was horrible and rudimentary to come to my uncle's gala, I declined his personal invitation to stay at his house, and it turns out that this hotel, the epitome of incompetence, doesn't have a room for me!"

"Miss, please keep calm."

"I will be forced to annoy my uncle to inform him how I am being treated and this hotel will suffer the consequences of your ineptitude," she says, pointing to the blonde.

A man no more than forty years old approaches the reception and with a voice as neat as his suit, tries to calm De Barbé's tacky niece.

"Miss, we understand your annoyance, I as Manager and on behalf of the hotel, offer you an apology and I beg you to be kind enough to stay with us in the presidential suite, of course, free of any charge," he says.

The chubby face of the girl can not avoid a huge smile of happiness, I don't know if it is because of the fact that she won't have to pay or because her scandal has borne fruit at the mere mention of Ramón de Barbé. Suddenly she turns to us, as if to make sure that she has more audience in that recognition made by the Hotel Manager. I can see how her arrogance is transformed into a child's nervousness when she meets the seductive gaze of Satiro, who in a very well-prepared act, projects a false grimace of admiration on his face.

Joshua continues talking to our receptionist, but I catch his sideways glance, Satiro smiles and the plan begins.

"One thing is for Reneé to send instructions to further complicate the plan and quite another is for us to complicate it ourselves," says Silfide, taking a bottle of water from the minibar in our suite. Satiro types something on his Nexus and it looks like a musician absorbed in a piano, playing the last piece of the night. He has that intense look that we regularly see in him.

"In fact," says Estirge "I think the plan proposed by Joshua and Sátiro is even simpler and easier than the one we drew up together with Reneé."

"It's a plan based on chance," says Drider, walking around the room, "the chance of having found Ramón de Barbé's niece here."

"That's what I mean" continues Silfide, "there are many risks of continuing to modify our initial plan."

"There are not as many changes," explains Joshua. "Reneé and Delonge wanted us to change our venue and stay here to be near the place where the Ramón de Barbé Gala will be held. There will be Alex Zendejas, Luis Romano and obviously Ramón, so, as Reneé had indicated in SyanL, the possibilities that Lola will attend this gala are huge", explains Joshua, projecting with his Nexus a map of the site where the event will be held, as well as a copy of the invitation that was made to Toot officials.

Our initial idea was to enter the party through emergency exits but the night before Dora Tarín had given interviews to the Kaoy media, informing that she would attend the Gala where her uncle would hold the annual Whiskey exhibition, that is why we are sure that Lola will attend. The discretion of that event had been maximum, it is not surprising that Ramón de Barbé's niece mentioned it with the intention of projecting herself as a guest at such an exclusive event among the political and business class of Toot.

We just found out about Dora's interview this morning, this twist has been so extreme that I haven't had time to even assimilate what happened, first with Drider and then with Estirge. I see them, they both check the projection of the map that Joshua presents. No one could see the way Estirge and I were kissing before dawn, except Ondina, who hasn't said a single word about it. I don't want her to, I want that moment to be between Estirge and me, nothing more, no one else. I'm still scared, but before that kiss I was afraid of losing something that I wasn't even sure I had. Now I feel more courageous, I don't know if it is because the time to carry out the mission is closer or because I am certain that after all these years, all this time, Estirge and I have a high point in our history, after being side by side, destroying for many years, killing for many years, today we have something to build. The only thing left for us is to survive.

"Actually, the presence of Ramón's niece makes everything easier. We will not have to infiltrate the Gala in the dark, because if we manage to get close to Dora Tarín de Barbé, we may be able to enter through the front door, without raising any suspicions. Once inside, we wait for the right moment and we eliminate the four of them, Alex, Ramón, Luis and of course Lola, just as Reneé and Delonge established it," indicates Joshua.

"The problem is that if we go through the front door, they will surely check us, scan us and we won't be able to have our weapons with us," says Ondina.

"That does not present any difficulty, the weapons will already be there, I have contacts that can hide them before the gala," Joshua responds with an impatient gesture that makes me think of Reneé, "once inside, we will get to work at a certain hour, and almost simultaneously to the actions we will meet on the roof of the place, the jet will be ready, ten minutes after starting the attack, I will contact the pilot to wait for us on time, it is very important to do things in just the right time to escape."

"I'm in charge of making *friendship* with Dora Tarín," indicates Sátiro "the gala is tomorrow night so I have all day today to work it," he mentions. Drider and Estirge smile knowingly. Dora Tarín is not a pretty or nice girl, on the contrary, her vulgar and arrogant appearance makes her even more unpleasant, but we could all realize her shock when meeting Sátiro's blue eyes.

"What if the whale doesn't take you into account?" Silfide asks, sounding contemptuous and jealous at the same time. It's absurd, she knows that Satiro will do it for the plan and that she, being so beautiful, doesn't have to be jealous of Dora. But that is precisely what happens with the two of them. In her relationship with Satiro, she does not see herself as the gorgeous woman that she is, but as another human being, almost like a girl, because what attracts Satiro to her, we all know, is not her face, nor her body, but everything she has kept since she joined us: her vulnerability, her uproarious laughter, her anger and tantrums, her lonely life in the refuge of the Saviors, and that Silfide knows well. Since he lost Lito, Satiro looks for someone to take care of and Silfide has always been that person.

"That's impossible," corrects Satiro "the woman who can be capable of rejecting me has not been born yet... you should know it," he says this last sentence lowering his voice, my friend looks at him furiously, "but in the unimaginable case that Dora Tarín is different from all women" he remarks, Silfide narrows her eyes, and sighs irritably before Satiro continues, "I suppose we can return to the plan of sneaking into the gala like nocturnal cats, right?", he asks, looking at Joshua.

"Indeed, but I don't think it will be necessary", says Joshua, "the idea that you seduce her is very solid."

"*Solid* the fucking mother who gave birth to that cow," Silfide murmurs, only I and Drider hear her. We looked at each other, holding on to laughter, just a second before we remembered the kiss he gave me the night before, in front of everyone and with terrible results. He seems to suddenly revive it, his big, sad eyes like those of an old dog drift away, and that old dog transforms into a young Doberman and looking with interest at Joshua, he speaks for the first time in several hours.

"The only thing left to do is to decide something fundamental: who will kill who".

CHAPTER

37

We went down to the coastal food restaurant in the hotel. Satiro is not coming with us. First he will pretend to be upset because according to our alibi, he's the only one who comes to Toot on vacation without a partner. For the rest of us, I hold Joshua's hand, Ondina comes with Drider and thanks to my suggestion, Silfide comes hugging Estirge. She is much prettier than Ondina but I don't trust the mermaid, I prefer Estirge to pretend to be a partner of someone I trust. He doesn't say it, but I know he prefers to see me next to Joshua, who from far and near is much more attractive than Drider. Besides Joshua didn't kiss me off guard in front of everyone, like Drider did.

The hotel, I have to accept it, is elegant even in the elevator attendant. The restaurant looks like something out of a movie about the antique nation of *Italy*. I look at Joshua out of the corner of my eye, elegant profile and a cute pink mouth, I think he's even cuter than any of the three of us girls. His carefree appearance is what attracts the most, he wears a two-day beard and his brown hair somewhat disheveled.

Estirge is very different, his hair is too unruly, not silky and manageable like my supposed partner's. We go downstairs and Joshua talks to our *maître*, who like the rest

196

of the staff, looks like a specimen from a catalog. I bet anything that all these people are not from Toot, they look like coastal and maybe they could even be from SyanL. Toot's people are not pretty, I could never fall in love with someone here. I look at Estirge, he wears the black suit with the elegance that can only come from SyanL. Beside him, Silfide in her tight red dress moves with the assurance that only the embodiment of beauty can show. The maître, with all his finesse and professionalism, cannot help but look at my friend. Luckily Satiro is not here yet to observe how the guys in the restaurant drole at Silfide.

We know that Dora Tarín will come down for dinner, we can assume it because her need to manifest herself as an influential person is evident, but we cannot take risks, Joshua has contacts at the hotel and they keep him informed. It is incredible how Joshua has become necessary for the mission, even though the guys did not receive him very well, now Joshua's contacts and ideas, as well as his leadership, have been very useful to us. Is that the reason for his presence? Do they have so little faith in us, Reneé and Delonge?

We arrive at the table of eight places, we are sure that Dora Tarín will not be the exception to the rule when it comes to Satiro's charm. Nobody is, no matter how much my feminine pride weighs on me, I have even had dreams of him, especially after that warm kiss a few years ago. I know my feelings, I know who is the only one who makes me think of whiskey ice as if they were river pebbles, who is the only one who makes me like that stupid melody, *La Vie en Rose*. I know it's Jimmy, but no woman can help feeling a tickle on her lips when meeting Satiro.

I don't know how I can be so sure of how I feel about Estirge, I just know that loving him, life is good fuel and that makes my fear of death not shine.

A waitress with a narrow waist and heart-shaped lips approaches to give us the menu, she does not hide when reviewing Joshua with her eyes, and there she should have stayed, but her eyes then go to Estirge. Well, congratulations on your quick debut to the slut category. She smiles at the person who matters most to me on this earth and offers him whiskey as if she were a nurse and he a war wounded. Silfide looks at me and guesses my jealousy, then winks at me and speaks.

"Sweetie" she says to the waitress, "is it possible that someone who looks less like a desperate spinster can serve us? Thank you" Silfide's voice puts an end to the waitress's flirtation, Estirge looks at my friend and then at me. He smiles, it's like he's kissing me again. That is enough for now.

"There is Dora," says Ondina taking a cigarette that Drider offers her. She does not generally smoke, but it is her habit to try to be more interesting than she really is , thinking that with cigarettes she will succeed.

Dora occupies the table in front of us, her reservation was made by Joshua's contacts. Ramón's niece orders a glass of rum and our antipathy further wins her over. Rum. Silfide smiles, the jealousy she may have felt earlier momentarily diluted by the drink Dora just ordered. Satiro has a disgust for rum, which serves to comfort Silfide, at least for now.

At our table we all order whiskey, and the new waiter is pleased about it. I'm tempted to order a glass of *Tino Tawrr* to remember my grandfather, but that would be risky, especially when a criminal citizen of Toot's enemy nation was suspected of being here at the airport.

I order local whiskey, Root's, being sure about the excess alcohol my drink will have. Dora Tarín looks at her Nexus and types, her plump face looks bored, at first glance you can read that she hates her life, that having a rich and powerful uncle in Toot is not enough for her to feel that her existence is worth something.

There is Satiro, coming in, but he doesn't look at us, he doesn't look at anyone and he goes straight to the bar. Without any intention of exaggerating, he looks better than usual, his hair looks impeccable, his blue suit contrasts to the golden brown of his hair and matches his eyes, Silfide makes a great effort for ignoring him.

"Poor guy" says Ondina in a very loud voice, thus beginning the comedy, "woman after woman and he still can't find the right one."

"But we're not to blame, right? We had these trip planned… What do you think, baby?" Silfide says in the same volume and approaching Estirge, "after all, he is your best friend."

"He's just sad," he replies. I distinguish how Dora Tarín looks at us discreetly and then directs her eyes to the bar, where Satiro is.

"It is not our responsibility," Joshua intervenes "he is no longer a child, he should not be looking for nonsense, but for someone who really understands him" the serious and pleasant tone of his voice makes this really seem like a casual conversation, between young people gossiping about a friend.

"I understand *you*, sweetie," I say with an idiotic voice. Joshua smiles at me and kisses me quickly on the lips. I can't help but look at Estirge, he smiles nonchalantly but takes a deep sip of his dry whiskey.

"Shall we order?" Drider asks, raising his voice. Dora Tarín looks at us openly, without hiding. I wish we could know what goes through her mind. We call the waiter to order, and she does the same. We don't see immediate progress on our plan, but we know it's no reason to despair, we have all night to make Dora to get closer to our friend in some way.

And so it happens, minutes later a waiter takes Satiro a double whiskey. We can see that it is a *Joan Megghia* whiskey, from SyanL because of the decoration of the glass in blue and gold, it is customary to decorate it with certain details, depending on the place of origin of the drink. Even though Dora Tarín is drinking rum, she knows that the most exquisite liquor in this place is SyanL's whiskey and that is why she sends it to Sátiro.

We see how the waiter offers Sátiro a delicate glass, and then whispers something in his ear. Satiro, playing his role well, pretends to be surprised and incredulous, he looks at Dora's table and smiles at her, raising his glass.

We know his next move ahead of time: he sends Dora the same thing, SyanL whiskey. Dora smiles and then looks at us.

"Can I sit with you? I am alone," she asks, smiling with the confidence she feels of having received Satiro's attention.

"It would be our pleasure," is Joshua who answers, with his easy mischievous smile. Two men like that, paying attention to a vulgar arrogant like she is, this girl must feel dreamed.

"Thank you!" she replies. I understand what she's doing, she wants Satiro to approach her on his own feet and she wants to get it through us. And that is precisely what we are looking for. Dora sits next to Joshua as the waiter brings her the drink, she leaves an empty spot in the chair next to her. Silfide's expressive eyes pierce her, she doesn't like that little act and we all know why. My friend is very professional and knows not to mix the personal in this, but even so, you never know what might happen. I feel it in my own flesh because Ondina is sitting next to Estirge and that weighs on me, especially because I don't know if I will be able to ignore her approaches to him, since she will surely have them throughout the evening. Joshua is supposed to be my partner for now and that's the only thing I should be interested in.

"Where are you from?" Asks Dora. Somehow her arrogance bothers me, at the table she is the least attractive of all and she moves and laughs as if it were not like that.

"We are from LaGem, all of us," indicates Joshua, "well, except for Jair, he is from La Costa," Joshua points him with his head before taking a drink of his whiskey. I can't help feeling uneasy about the fact that we're using our real names, but we have no option, those names appear on our fake IDs, only changing the place of origin.

"Oh, I have never visited LaGem, I am not a mountain person, you know?" she addresses only him, "I am totally from the city."

"LaGem is also an urban place, although it is surrounded by mountains," Silfide points out , which alerts me, this is the behavior we don't need. We require this woman to love us and invite us to the Ramón de Barbé gala.

"I know," she answers, apparently she did not notice the fury in Silfide's voice, "but as for the cosmopolitan, none compares to Toot, I suppose you will agree, now that I live in Kaoy for studies, I have proven, Toot is unique," she says looking directly at the bar. Satiro is still sitting there, turning his back to us, as if he didn't know anything. Dora is dying to drop the formalities and ask about him.

"Are you on vacation?" He looks at us, now, at all of us.

"Yes, although this hotel doesn't make justice to Toot's fame" says Drider, putting on his biggest face of distaste. Dora's face lights up.

"Right? It's terrible, at least I'm not used to this kind of treatment," she replies, snapping her fingers in a rude way, the waiter approaches, "another and take one more to the young man at the bar," she says, emboldened.

"Of course, anything else?" He looks at us, he is extremely attractive, he has dark hair, big green eyes.

"I can think of a couple of things ..." Silfide says, winking at him, we all laugh, including him. The only one who doesn't seem to find it funny is Dora. When the waiter leaves, she expresses her opinion.

"Why do you flirt with the servants? And in front of your boyfriend!" she looks at Estirge with a worried gesture. Damn, it's true, we are all supposed to be here as a couple, except Satiro.

"It doesn't matter," answers Estirge, shrugging "in the end she goes with me, not with the waiter" he says, thank goodness, good answer, although imagining what he said is not exactly pleasant for me, even when I know that it is a sham.

"And why isn't your friend from the bar with you?" Dora asks while nervously playing with a golden napkin.

"Ah!" I answer with the gesture that a mother would make complaining about her son, "he is upset, we are all supposed to come as a couple, but before leaving ..." I drink a little of my whiskey enjoying Dora's impatient face, "he found out his girlfriend was cheating on him. He arrived at the airport and after telling us what had happened ..."

"He decided that he would come alone to the trip," continues Silfide "he had been lucky to get rid of the woman he was dating" I observe her, maybe it's just my perception, but I can't help but notice that soft note in Silfide's voice when she talks about Satiro. It has always been difficult for me to understand their relationship, but I know it is not easy. The two of them carry a tough past. What happened with Sátiro's brother, Lito, seems like a comedy chapter compared to the rest of his story and I mean the story of both. Perhaps that is why they are each other's favorite, their lives are so broken that they have already formed a puzzle between the two. I don't know if putting the pieces together like this is going to work for them.

It seems that Dora Tarín does not notice at all the affectionate tone in my friend's voice, she just looks at Satiro, who is still at the bar, alone.

"There is no human life that can bring him, he is obstinate" I finish, Dora looks at him intrigued, Satiro's appearance creates curiosity, but this time, it is not his thin lips; what attracts Barbé's niece is his anger, his apparent disappointment and vulnerability. Or at least that is what she believes, since the least vulnerable person I have met in my life is Satiro, however, she doesn't know.

"What do you think if..." Dora begins, however she is unable to complete her question, because Ondina interrupts.

"Jimmy, do you have a lighter?" she says to Estirge as she casually touches his arm, she can't be that stupid! I'm sure Dora was going to get Satiro. Also I don't like the way she addresses Estirge or the way she touches him. She knows what happens between us, she was the only one who saw us this morning, I know she does it with the intention of annoying me.

"Eh, no, sorry," he answers, uncomfortable. I smile when Dora narrows her eyes and insists.

"As I was saying before being interrupted by your cigar addiction," she tells Ondina and I can't help but widen my smile, it's inevitable, "what do you think if one of you talk to him?" she looks at Satiro almost childishly, "I am so sorry that he is there alone and we are here, having such a good time!" Dora has ordered another rum and her cheeks are flushed. She prides herself on being fine and important, but a few shots of ordinary rum make her blush.

"Why don't you go, sweetie?" She says to Estirge and all the sympathy that her rudeness to Ondina had provoked in me, vanishes when I see her giving orders to Estirge. I watch him smile forcibly, I know that at this moment he would love to put this spoiled woman in her place, but he gets up and with that cute gesture on his lips, goes to the bar where Satiro continues drinking. I see him go through the restaurant, I like the ease and harmony with which he moves, it seems that he takes the role of the young heir that he is playing very seriously.

Dora Tarín's nervous gaze also follows him, she knows that if Sátiro says no, the rejection would be towards her and such a person is not used to that type of humiliation. Estirge asks the bar manager for something, according to the glass I know it's SyanL whiskey. I imagine the taste of that whiskey in his mouth and I have to close my eyes so I don't run to kiss him one more time. He sits down next to Satiro and they both turn to our table. Dora blushes even more when Satiro smiles at her. Silfide drinks the contents of her own drink extremely quickly. And then I understand it, I see it clearly: she is mortally in love with him. Several moments pass through my head: the day that Satiro found her in the middle of the main avenue with a broken wrist, she had just escaped from the shelter and the class B agents who caught her, gave her a severe beating, They wanted something more, but he arrived on time, along with Jimmy, making the attackers flee. Also on that occasion when Satiro almost died from the wound in his abdomen, Silfide was the only one who spent three nights awake taking care of him. When my friend traveled to Mahat to get the Dali virus that would kill the four beetles, Satiro went to pick her up at the airport, the flight arrived at five in the morning and they had checked in until three in the afternoon. Nobody ever asked them where they were, or what had happened, it is ridiculous how the love of others passes in front of your eyes and you do not see it because you are so immersed in your own. Now I see it so clearly, Silfide knows that this is a ruse but still does not resist jealousy, even from a woman like Dora who could never mean something to Satiro.

Estirge and I are not the only ones who feel that fear of losing someone. I see how Dora doesn't take her eyes off the bar. The gestures that Estirge makes, convincing Satiro seem real, he looks at us and smiles. Dora knows that she has won, that he will be here soon. It's hard to blame that glee.

They both come to the table, Satiro is slightly taller than Estirge, but both move gracefully, the sad face he pretends to show is almost sexy, almost morbid. As expected, he sits next to Dora, smiling shyly.

"Thanks for the whiskey," Satiro says directly, greeting her with a kiss on the cheek and hugging her a little. Silfide's gaze follows all those movements. I understand my friend, I understand that although Dora is inferior to her in every way and level, it is impossible for her not to squirm with jealousy, and perhaps that is the worst thing: seeing the person you love with someone who makes him look withered and boring. I look at Ondina, who as always tries to get Estirge's attention. Yes, definitely seeing the person you love with the embodiment of boredom, is frustrating.

"Don't even mention it, I know how to recognize when someone needs a detail," Dora touches him on the shoulder.

"What makes you think that I ...?" He looks confused and looks at us, "no, no, you guys can't be so nosy and go around talking about my life!" he says and then looks at her, "you idiots make me look bad with this pretty lady," he smiles.

I can't believe Dora is such an idiot as to fall for that. But she is.

"Look bad? What do you mean?" she asks. For her we no longer exist, we are a simple frame that surrounds her flirtation with him, who only winks in response. Silfide calls the waiter and asks for SyanL whiskey, this time neat. She drinks it like this only when she's nervous or upset. Dora continues talking to Satiro and the rest of us have to talk among ourselves, it would be suspicious to remain watching them like idiots. Either way, I know Joshua will be quietly listening to every word of their conversation. I turn to Silfide, who has just finished the whole drink and is already calling the waiter to order another.

"Sweetie, another please, neat," she says touching the waiter in the arm, Satiro turns around and looks at her strangely, even amused. The waiter returns with Silfide's whiskey and this is the most dangerous moment of the whole night, as Satiro does not resist and speaks:

"I thought you didn't drink it neat," he says. Dora stops smiling and watches them both, frowns, puzzled. My nerves grow, it is a type of intimacy that cannot be hidden. A heavy silence invades the table and I look at Estirge, in his eyes I see the clear apology for what he will do. I nod discreetly and look at the bottom of my glass, so I don't see what is about to happen, however, I do hear Estirge's voice.

"She drinks it like that because I find it very sexy," he says and then follows a silence where I know he is kissing her.

CHAPTER

38

"I hate all this," says Silfide in a low voice, "I hate this woman and Lola, and everyone, I hate Reneé and Delonge," she laughs bitterly, "I hate that today may be the last day of my life," she look at her glass of water with nostalgia. We both tried to ignore the bustle at the table "I hate not being able to drink more whiskey on this, my last night."

"If we drink more, tomorrow we will go to a direct failure," I tell her, even though I'm feeling the same as her.

"It's strange, I don't know if it's a thing of bringing SyanL's spirit deep inside, but when I drink whiskey I forget that I'm capable of complaining, crying or getting angry" through the large window you can see the orange sunset of Toot, full of buildings" I only remember looking at the horizon and its colors" she sighs.

"Toot is horrible" I say, "but a sunset is beautiful from anywhere."

"I can't believe the last person he's going to be with before what could be our last day of life is that spoiled brat," she says, watching Satiro talking to Dora.

"It's time to go," interrupts Estirge, I see him and the words *last day* echo in my head "come on," he says in a low voice, "Satiro will stay here with Dora, from then on, he will manage this alone," he explains to us. Joshua also comes over and takes my hand.

"Satiro wants us to leave them alone, he has her eating out of his hand," he says, I see them and I realize that his comment is literal, Dora takes a piece of creamy cookie that he offers her, he has his charming smile of a teenager in love.

I look at Silfide carefully, she is suffering a lot. Yes, it is better that we go to sleep at once, tomorrow Sátiro will inform us if we are going to the Ramón de Barbé gala or if we will have to slip into it. Estirge takes Silfide by the hand, and somehow it seems he is offering his condolences.

Ondina and Drider get up together with us and we say goodbye. We have a plan based in Satiro's charm. I'm not worried, I know he will succeed, it is tomorrow that makes me nervous. The six of us are in the elevator, the only one speaking is Silfide.

"It's absurd, ridiculous and I think that he is crossing the line, he does not have to behave like a husband with the pregnant woman, right? Satiro is exaggerating!"

"Calm down," Joshua tells her, "he knows what he's doing."

"I got the impression that Tarín fell into the trap," Drider intervenes "she looked more than pleased with Sátiro's cloying pampering.

"And surely they were just beginning," says Ondina, with a half-smile, to Silfide's irritation.

"I do not want to know, I am not interested," interrupts Silfide, straight away.

"Don't be such a baby girl" Drider scolds her, we all know Silfide's feelings, but it's the kind of topic we never touch on and Drider chooses this moment to speak it aloud, "emotions have to be restricted in these cases."

"Oh, really?" Estirge speaks, with his ironic tone, looking at Drider in a questioning way, "Is it true? Are the feelings left out?" His voice is the only thing that is heard along with the noise of the elevator, at this time of night, there is hardly anyone in the lobby.

"If you refer to the moment I had with Gorgona" Drider replies contemptuously as we go up, his tone of voice bothers me and I feel that there is something very embarrassing in all this, "it was not important," he ends.

"Wasn't it?" Ondina asks, mocking and incredulous at the same time, in the reflection of the elevator. Drider looks at me and then at Estirge.

"It was a stupid impulse" he says resolutely, "I am scared of death" his eyes darken, "it is something we are all feeling," he looks at us, I see that Joshua approves with a gesture of resignation, "we are all scared of what will happen tomorrow, don't you feel it, Estirge?" he interrogates him with that hard look. We have reached the floor of our rooms. In Drider's pupils I can see a bitter poison, emulating the spider that is his symbol, "don't you suddenly feel like doing stupid things? Things…actions, so absurd that you've never done before, until this precise moment," he continues, his gesture is transformed now in outrage.

Then I understand. We stop outside the elevator, no one intends to move, I feel the tension growing even more, what happened a while ago, at the table in the presence of Dora, was nothing compared to this environment. Ondina crosses her arms and looks at me without blinking, she is already smiling openly. Her face is no what it used to be; she used to look at me differently, almost with admiration, she used to be aware of my words, my gestures and on many occasions, she imitated me, now her gaze is full of resentment, and it is mixed with a very twisted enjoyment at this scene. So I understand that she told Drider, she told him that she saw us kissing the same night he kissed me. Estirge does not respond, he has understood everything.

"Well?" Drider insists. Somehow it bothers me that his sudden kiss meant nothing.

"Nothing I've done in these days causes me regret," I feel Estirge's hand take mine, my first thought is that Dora Tarín could see us and the plan would be ruined. Then I am aware of the warm contact of his fingers, of his hands…those hands that have killed, that have fired goldguns, copperguns, silverguns a million times, his hands that have strangled, stabbed and now they feel soft, firm between mine.

Ondina and Drider look at us, right now there is a rivalry between us that feels similar to the eternal competition that there has always been between SyanL and Toot.

Joshua has remained silent, I guess he is studying the situation. Silfide didn't even know we stopped and she must be in the room by now.

"Lucky you," Drider replies.

"And you can't even imagine how" it seems that Estirge has no intention of ending this discussion either.

"Enough" Joshua speaks, finally, "Estirge and Drider, I want to see you in my room. Now" his tone of leader, makes a dent even in two voracious cold-blooded assassins like them. Joshua walks and Drider follows him, annoyed at having to obey orders at such an intense and personal moment. Estirge squeezes my hand and looks at me warmly before following Joshua. My insides ache to see him walk away. When you feel the danger on your neck, kissing the back of your neck, the cold breath of fear at dusk, something that is needed is the closeness of the most important person in your life. I start to walk towards the room when I remember that I am not alone, Ondina holds my arm.

"I need to talk to you."

CHAPTER

39

We don't to any of the rooms. So I suppose this conversation has to be private. We walk a few meters until we reach a luxurious and crystalline room, like the rest of the hotel. It looks like a boardroom. There are black armchairs surrounding a hall and beyond it a blue glass table. In the wide windows you can see Toot at night. The lights of the buildings have an almost impossible symmetry, along the urban landscape lines are formed between the buildings, but a disturbing silence surrounds them. Toot sleeps completely, the workers of the city never stay up late, because they live according to a system that tells them to sleep eight hours at night without interruption and half an hour in the afternoon to regain strength. It is important for Lola Tehran government that its citizens work after they have had enough rest. And that's how Toot's night view projects it: silent and peaceful. Ondina closes the door behind her and sits nonchalantly in one of the black armchairs. I do the same in an adjoining armchair but I avoid her gaze, I scan the walls and windows.

"Well?" I say, now looking at my Nexus, downplaying that awkward moment.

"I know what you want to do," she says, "about Estirge, I know you want to protect him, I overheard your conversation with Satiro on the plane," she confesses. I smile wryly.

"Do you go through life listening other people's talks?" I laugh cruelly, "mine, especially!"

"I pay attention to what I care about," she continues with the same seriousness, her face is mistreated, acne again invades her skin and the scar on her cheek has acquired an ashy appearance, "and Estirge matters a lot to me" sentence, "I have always cared about him."

A bitter feeling weighs on my stomach, it is difficult to ignore this jealousy and this desire to disappear from here.

"Thank you for your concern," I answer, standing up "but *we* don't need it," I emphasize the plural to make it clear, to make clear that the relationship that matters is ours, Estirge's and mine, nobody else's.

"And tell me then, how do you plan to save him? How do you plan to prevent a tragedy from happening to him? You have never been able to do it before with other people," she says, touching a fiber of my very intense past, which I prefer to ignore "I also remind you that this was your cause, it was the death of the Executor that put us in this situation," she affirms, opening her arms, as if wanting to encompass all of Toot.

"It's not true, it was fortuitous. Delonge himself told us that the SyanL government has followed our trail for years," I reply. Ondina laughs uproariously, the sound of her fake attention-hungry laughter running through my blood.

"You really are naïve…with that tiny brain you intend to save Jimmy?" She says.

"Don't call him by his real name."

"I'm calling him the way I want to do it! You're not its fucking owner, damn it!" she exclaims, spitting out a few drops of saliva that fall on my arm. I need my biggest reserve of patience to stay here, holding it, "I'm already tired of this secrecy, I'm done with the private meetings, what are they for anyway?"

"I have no idea what you're talking about," I say and it's true, I don't know what she means, maybe she's already gone crazy. She takes a deep breath, like trying to be unflappable.

"Well, I needed to talk to you because I don't want something to happen to Estirge either. I care in the same way as you do and even when I know that maybe he doesn't give a damn, because I am not the girl he wants, nor do we like the same music and I don't read like you or him. I understand it, I understand the reasons why he prefers to be with you," she continues with her arms crossed and she doesn't even dare to look at me while she says all that. I know the reality is that she doesn't understand anything. Nothing at all: Estirge and I have a history, full of all the range of emotional tones that may exist and that she will never understand. Maybe because she has never experienced it.

"Where do you want to go with all of this?" I finally say.

"If you want to protect Estirge, I can help you, I can do what Satiro didn't want to do."

"How?" I don't deny that it brings curiosity to me and that in order to prevent something terrible from happening to Estirge, I am able to ally myself with the darkest being of any nation.

"I'll keep an eye on him, that's what I can do, follow in his footsteps during the fun moment when we go to the gala. Nothing will happen to him, you have my word," he promises, "and if you see the need to require my help, let me know, I will do whatever it takes, in order to protect him."

I know she cares about him. I've always known, I know she has to deal with that every day. With the fact of living knowing he doesn't feel the same.

"Why are you doing this, Ondina?" I insist, waiting for her to say that the reason is something else.

"You...mean something for him. I don't. The only choice I have to be relevant for him, is by saving his life."

I can make out five in the morning on my Nexus when I hear the bedroom door slowly close, I reach out and take the goldgun from the nightstand, with a quick movement I throw myself to the floor and point to the door.

"It's me," says Silfide's voice. I blink several times and can then I see her silhouette. After turning on the light and I see her clearly. She wears white shorts and a sleeveless shirt to sleep. She approaches, flopping onto my bed while I remain on the floor of the room, in the same defensive position, holding my weapon.

"It's horrible," she says, I don't know what she means, at this moment everything could be.

"Where were you?" I ask, putting the goldgun back on the table.

"I have been with Satiro," she sinks his face into the pillow and the mass of long red hair is in disarray.

"Didn't he go with Dora?

"Yes, but the whale is sleeping," she looks at me. Her eyes don't reflect the happiness of someone who has been with the person she loves.

"Are you okay?" I insist.

"No, but this is not about whether I'm okay, are you?" she blurts out.

"Why shouldn't I be?" I say crossing my arms.

"Is there anything you want to tell me?

"No."

"Are you sure?"

"I don't know what you're talking about," I say, I look at my Nexus and go online, out of habit. There is nothing new on any platform.

"Yes, you do"

"We are always looking for something weird in every situation, in every moment…it is very SyanL" I answer, leaning back, "but yes something happened," I finally give in, "it is about him."

"About Estirge?" Silfide smiles, her curly hair framing her heart-shaped face. I can't help but smile at the memory as well, and if we're going to die tomorrow, we deserve a while of healthy frivolity.

"Yes," I say, I doubt if I should be talking about it, because I have not discussed it with him, but I see my friend's expression and I can tell that she has the urge to forget about

Satiro for a moment, so I smile and tell her. The words come out of my mouth and it seems that I relive everything. I relive his close face, his warm face, his mouth flavored with grapes and apple, like a drip of Joan Megghia, SyanL's most representative whiskey.

Suddenly I remember the dream I was having before Sílfide woke me up: the strange images mixed with the memory of what I am telling her, I see both Estirge's face and his lips approaching, but also the images of an avenue, a place completely lonely and long… they cross my head. I was lost in the darkness of the city, crossing the street , walking by the cars, being chased by someone I don't know, without any weapon that could provide me protection. This I have already lived, that dream of tonight that now fills my head, pushing the memory of Estirge's kisses, I embodied it once or many times. I'm not sure now.

"Gorgona?" Silfide's voice brings me back to reality so suddenly that I feel dizzy when my eyes fall back on the white sheet. I hadn't really looked anywhere else, it was my mind that was absent.

"Yeah, sorry, I got lost," I say, trying to sound nonchalant.

"It doesn't matter, I understand what he means to you, what he has meant from the moment he entered your life. I imagine you must feel a shock of emotions, right?" shee looks at me, sadly, " to know that is *now*, precisely now that finally ..." She stops, she knows that she should stop and that's fine. I don't want to hear the possible ending of that sentence either. I am scared. I'm scared because of him.

"I was born with all the violence in the world around me and that has made me capable of the best and the worst, what weighs on me is that both are encapsulated in this period of time that is so short, that life has put them so" an incredulous laugh escapes from me, and I know there is nothing more to add.

CHAPTER

41

Joshua needs three teaspoons of sugar in his coffee. First he puts one on it, dissolves it and then licks the tip of the spoon, then he takes more sugar and repeats the action, he does it with patience and elegance, he turns the fact of drinking coffee into a complete ritual, almost as much as in what whiskey refers to any bar in SyanL. I watch him from the entrance to the hotel restaurant. It is 7:20 in the morning and outside Toot's sky is gray, the drops of the thick rain that only is common at this time of year, slide quickly, they don't hit the glass gently, on the contrary, they rush, like resembling the same trouble we feel.

Joshua is the only one in the hotel restaurant, he reads the newspaper and his sportswear as if he had just been exercising gives the impression of a warmth that makes me think of home, in the desire to forget everything, I don't refer only to these days, but to everything that has been my life.

For a moment I imagine that my false identity is real: that I was born in LaGem and that I am a student, that my only future concern would be to find a job, but no, no, no, instantly a guilt runs through my head, no. This is my life, my destiny, I will never complain of being born in SyanL, it is my country and I am proud of that, despite its crime, its economic depressions, its natural disasters, its inept rulers and the violence of which I am also part of. I was born in SyanL, the most chaotic nation on the planet, many would say that it is the worst place to be born. And I will probably die in Toot, which many would say is the best place to die.

One sector of Toot has around two hundred retirement homes where the elderly from both here and from other nations come to live their last days, away from the hustle and bustle. Despite having a reputation for being an enviable resort, full of peace and spirituality, there is not a single person from SyanL. They die at home, they are buried in the same crypt as the rest of their family, or are cremated and placed in the same niche as their parents and grandparents. SyanL elders like to die in their homes or in their workplaces, they do not say goodbye to their land to go to die in an artificial paradise.

Joshua sees me and raises his hand, asking me to come closer. In the restaurant a soft jazz is heard that somehow sounds morning. On one side of the restaurant there is a tall counter with a wide variety of wild fruits, pops up the pink guava, typical of the Toot region. I'm not hungry. When I sit across from Joshua, the waiter immediately fills my cup of hot coffee, Joshua thanks him with a smile and he leaves.

"Everything has gone well," he announces to me, his brown hair even at this time of the morning looks perfect,

"Ramón's niece has bitten and has even chewed the hook at will, in fact she does not want to let go of it for a minute," he explains, making a disgusted face, "Satiro has guts and stomach," he says, I nod with a slight smile, I don't feel like talking, it's somehow annoying, I would regularly laugh and spice up the conversation with more taunts about Dora Tarín, but now I think there is enough poison in our group to intensify it further. Joshua notices it.

"Well, we will go to the Gala today, that is a fact. We'll meet later to outline the plan and put the finishing touches," he drinks some of the steaming, dark liquid. Joshua is very attractive, just like the others. I think that of the four, Estirge is perhaps the least conspicuous, not because he is not worthy, but because Satiro, Drider and Joshua are way too attractive. I wish Ondina would fall in love with one of them.

"However," Joshua continues, "I needed to talk to you first," I am surprised by the coldness with which his angelic face suddenly turns hard.

"I'm here."

"This plan is spontaneous and difficult, Gorgona, therefore we cannot allow ourselves to go around with school fights and childish things that are not at all typical of people like you."

"What do you mean by *people like you*?" I ask, although I can guess what he means.

"Murderers, thugs, criminals," he says, sipping his coffee. There is some accusation in his voice, it is the second conversation I have with him in private, I remember that the first time he was kinder, but can he really be blamed? His life is in the same danger as ours and he wouldn't even have to be here.

"Can I ask you a question?" I look directly into his limpid honey eyes, he raises his eyebrows, waiting for my question to come out suddenly.

"Who are you? What are you doing? Why are you here?" I say, Joshua smiles at me.

"Those were three questions, darling," his reproving tone reminds me of someone, despite having softened his response with the tender compliment.

"I know, but they mean the same thing," I insist, "why the hell are you on this mission, fighting for something that doesn't concern you? Risking your life with six strangers whom you have a few days of meeting?

"I'm not here for fun," he says smiling. His smile shocks me for some reason.

"Well, fuck Delonge!" And Reneé!, fuck that plastic president and that arrogant whore!" I say, trying to keep the volume of my voice low.

"You hit the nail on the head, it's because of her I'm here, she asked me to be, that arrogant whore."

"And are you his lap dog or his lover?" I fold my arms and he stands up, ready to leave. He approaches, tucks my hair behind my ear and without removing that cynical smile, he leaves.

It's not just me. I see the world around and I perceive it badly. No hope, no places to run away and hide. Toot has always been a cold city, the whole planet knows that, even the similarity of the buildings is disturbing, straight and impassive.

Inside me, I shudder to believe that Toot will have a domino effect, once we bring Lola down, these perfect buildings and their entire system will fall one by one. I see my reflection in the glass of my bedroom window. The long green dress is too stretched to my body but it is not a big problem, since I have executed missions with even more uncomfortable clothes, although never as complicated as this. My hair falls in a chestnut cascade on the side of my face, I don't know if this outfit is discreet enough, but it's Joshua's instructions and the dress is shipped directly from him, as well as the clothes from the rest of us. My neck is not nude, I wear my hanging with the snake.

I sigh, a round yellow moon floats over this soulless city, and I have the feeling that this sky is the most beautiful image I will see tonight. Will this be the last moon of my life? I will probably not be here tomorrow to see another one.

"Can I?" Estirge's voice makes me turn around as I see him enter the room. I can't help but smile to see him like this, in a perfect black tuxedo, without a blemish, without a single wrinkle. Internally I pray that throughout the night his clothes continue the same, without any stain, without anything to indicate that he has been injured. I hate that image and I erase it from my head as quickly as it arrives. A fear stuck in my throat keeps me from breathing for a moment, but he reaches out and takes my hand. There is no fear in his gaze, but a kind of nostalgia, he holds my hand and with the other arm he surrounds my waist, drawing me closer to him.

"You are a beautiful way to show how ugly is the world we live in" he says and smiles.

"I'm not sure that's a compliment" I respond; he laughs and the sound of that laugh, almost hollow and deep makes me forget all the anguish contained. When that sound stops and all that's left are his eyes, to some inches from my face, I think how unfair it all is. SyanL is full of corrupt politicians, kidnappers, bad people and despite this, it is us, six young people, who have a marked destiny. I know it's something we chose, knowing that one day this would happen. I had nothing to lose in those years, because I had already lost the most important thing, until I met him.

"Jimmy," I tell him, using his real name, I feel like crying, but arriving like a woman in mourning at Ramón de Barbé's gala is not the best thing to do. But kissing him, that I can do and that's what I go for. I take his head and bring him closer to me, so fast that at the movement, his nose hits mine and it hurts, although only for a second, then it is as if I plunge into his mouth, it is as if the rest of my body is gone , I feel nothing but the softness of his lips and the caresses of his teeth, I like to know that this kiss seals everything, life, death, Toot's moon, SyanL's whiskey, the memories lounging behind me head, what is happening , all the things that will change, the place that we cannot redeem, that we cannot take revenge on. I run my hands over his face and it feels warm and soft. If I were Medusa, if I really had snakes on my head, I would hug him with them, protecting him; I would look at him and turn it to stone, to stay that way for eternity.

The knocks on the door make us separate. Ondina and Silfide enter the room.The dress of the first one is pale purple, the fabric looks quite coarse and I don't understand. Joshua is supposed to have chosen the entire wardrobe, I don't understand why he designated such an ugly dress for her. Ondina knows it, she looks upset and although she has never had the best taste, that pale color makes her look sick.

Sílfide is a different situation: her dress is short and cute, it reaches to her knee, but the fabric of this one makes her white and slender legs stand out, the rest of the garment adheres to her waist and then I understand Joshua's idea: he doesn't want us to look the same, he doesn't want us to be associated with each other, that's why the clothing styles are that different, it amazes me how he works down to the smallest detail and that provides a certain confidence, that a plan so well drawn, even if spontaneous, cannot go wrong.

"What hour Joshua said we would have to be ready?" Ondina asks, trying to feel comfortable with her dress. She doesn't succeed and she has a point, because it's awful.

"At nine o'clock," I take the opportunity to check my Nexus and Estirge smoothes the sleeves of the suit that wrinkled when hugging me a moment ago.

"Don't we have to wait for the others?" Asks Silfide, checking her own lips, using the window glass as a mirror. Estirge responds focused and confident as always.

"No, Joshua and Drider are reviewing the last details of the plan, which we have already reviewed ad nauseam: Joshua, Drider, Satiro and I will go up to the second floor with your help, Silfide," she nods, rolling her eyes, annoyed to hear the same instruction over and over again "and you will be left in the place of the unfortunate guard who until that moment had been guarding the staircase. As you know, the second floor balcony will be where Lola will give her speech, as every time she steps on an event of any kind, she will only be accompanied by Alex Zendejas, who is an important figure in the meeting, Luis Romano, her head of security. and personal guard, and obviously Ramón, host of the event. Ondina and Gorgona remain on the first floor for eventualities, once the… *matter* is concluded, you girls go up protecting yourselves with your weapons and we leave the place"

"Only one thing," Silfide looks at him as if he were the culprit of all her misfortunes, "Where is Satiro? " she asks. Estirge, Ondina and I glanced at each other. We know the answer and even she knows it herself, but for some twisted reason she wants to hear it out loud. Estirge, despite being the cold-blooded murderer that he is, is noble with those he loves and hesitates to say a word. On the contrary, Ondina anticipates:

"He's with her, Silfide, you have to suffer this time, that's how it happens, we are not always with who we want to be," she says. It bothers me to know that with her words she refers to herself wanting to be with Estirge, but that is something that I can ignore now without any problem, since the mission that brought us here is getting closer and closer and I must not let anything distract me. I'm not sure that Silfide is following the same philosophy and what she says below confirms it:

"I'm going to kill her." Her gaze, far from being empty, fills with a kind of resentment that I'm sure we've all reflected at some time. I know what she means, I know whom she means, the three of us know it and even so, Estirge, true to his personality of seeing the iota of goodness in everyone, asks:

"Who are you talking about, Lola?

"No," replies my best friend, full of rage, a gesture that makes her look even more attractive, "I'm talking about Dora, the bitch who dared to touch my man..." and after saying this, she smiles and leaves the room. It is nine o'clock.

"Are you crazy?" Ondina looks more nervous than ever, pulling Silfide by the arm as we walk down the hall. "We have a mission, which I remind you of is not for pleasure, nor for money, we came here to kill Lola, the president," she says, making sure to lower her voice "that was the negotiation with Delonge in exchange of our lives, don't you remember?" she insists and even though I can't support her, she's right. Estirge looks at me uneasily, he doesn't know what to do about Silfide either. As we got on the elevator, we luckily found Joshua and Drider.

"Ah, just in time" says Ondina with a look of relief. In the elevator there is only our colleagues. As soon as the elevator door closes, Ondina speaks:

"We have a situation here," she goes to Joshua, who looks at her as if he saw an angry and unhinged mother-in-law. Ondina continues: "Silfide has decided that it is more important to kill Dora Tarin, out of jealousy, of course, rather than using that energy with Lola Teheran!" Joshua's gaze now rests on Silfide who remains impassive since she has already made the decision.

"Is that true?" He asks her without flinching. Sílfide purses her pink lips and nods, crosses her arms, as if challenging him.

"Very good," continues Joshua, taking out his Nexus, "you are out of mission."

"What?"

"No," says Estirge, "you cannot leave her out, we have a plan in which we are all involved, it is too late to change it, Joshua, you know what I mean," I look at Estirge, with some bewilderment, but I don't have time to ask anything.

"I can't risk the plan by having an emotional issue interfering," he says, we all look at each other, it's absurd, there are thousands of issues of this kind between us.

"I won't go anywhere," Silfide speaks suddenly, we are about to reach the ground floor of the hotel, "I'm going to kill that bitch and neither you, Joshua, nor any of you are going to stop me, we have known each other for many years and you all would do the same, you would act the same if you were in my place," her eyes release sparks and a thin layer of tears begins to form in them, we go on the third floor.

"No, that's a lie, I have felt everything you are living now," Drider begins, I look at him, he has a mature and honest gesture, "for a long time and the person who stands in my way is still alive," he follows.

I feel my heart beat strong, his eyes fall on Estirge, who holds his gaze.

"In fact that person is now breathing this same air," Drider inhales as if he is smelling a whiskey just taken from the barrel. It makes me think of my grandfather for a moment.

The elevator stops and the door opens, the image of Dora kissing Satiro is the first thing that appears before our eyes. Silfide takes Estirge's hand to continue the farce of couples we have formed. I feel Joshua's hand on my waist. Nothing can be done or changed, it's too late, I don't know at what time of the night, but Dora will die too. Drider and Ondina hold hands, I see them out of the corner of my eye and they look at each other, I see solidarity in their gesture and that worries me.

CHAPTER

44

The limousine is spacious and although its interior is overflowing with luxury, you can feel that coldness, that square sense that surrounds everything in Toot. It has the kind of elegance that a hearse would have.

"We have news for you," Dora says suddenly, her hands with golden nails intertwine with Satiro's.

"Oh, no my love, I think it would be better to leave it to the end of the night" he observes, looking at her with sweetness.

"What news?" asks Silfide, I understand her, I understand her jealousy, her stomach pain, her desire to cry, her desire to beat her head until she is unconscious and forget these images, her desire to hate, to insult, to destroy . I have felt it.

"Jair will move in with me!" she exclaims and kisses him. Although Silfide knows that this is part of the charade to get Dora to invite us to this party, her jealousy is perceived in the atmosphere.

"Congratulations!" Joshua says, he puts his hand on my leg, "a thousand times we have thought about taking that step, right?" He looks at me, trying to distract Silfide, diverting the uncomfortable conversation and it is fine. Which is not fine at all, are the eyes of Estirge scrutinizing Joshua's hand that is caressing on my bare thigh.

"Yes, of course, many times," I answer and take his hand, thus avoiding his direct contact with my skin. Estirge's eyes don't seem satisfied with it, but I'm nervous and don't feel like dealing with that feeling. Not now. I look at Ondina, she has her eyes fixed on Toot's landscape. I remember that of all the occasions when I saw her approaching Estirge, when I saw her hugging him or hinting at some intimacy that only exists in her head, he did not lift a finger so that I would not feel that anger. The thought hits me like a cold shower would in December and I don't understand why now I must worry about Estirge's feelings when, at similar times, he never cared about mine. I feel the adrenaline rush inside me, I close my eyes and a throbbing headache starts pounding in the back of my skull. This is not the time to be distracted, not now, not a few minutes from entering Ramón de Barbé's mansion, not a few hours away of ending this nightmare.

The atmosphere is very heavy, it seems as if suddenly, we had run out of oxygen, as if we no longer wanted to exist. We all have that empty, hollow look, the only one who does not have it, is Dora, could it be that it is the prelude to certain death? I look at Estirge's face and focus on his lips, they always seem to be ready for something: talking, kissing, smiling, cursing. I close my eyes again and try to review the location of my weapon in my head. Drider installed in our Nexus a guide to the location of each of our goldguns within the Gala, mine is in Ramón's meetings room, where the tracking of my Nexus will guide me without any failure.

"We're here!" Dora's hoarse and festive voice automatically turns our heads toward the elegant building in front of which the limousine pulls up. At first glance it looks like a government house, made of fine and neat marble, perhaps brought from LaGem. It has a wide and majestic arch in the front gate and the dark mahogany almost black door creates a majestic and clean contrast, it is as if Ramón wants to clarify to Toot that he should be their ruler and not Lola. I don't know how the President takes the fact that Ramón's properties probably outnumber her own homes.

I take Joshua's arm and study the surroundings. The area is deserted, except for the fancy cars that keep coming. I spot about ten cars of Toot's Police Officer and Land Force Lieutenants on nearby corners. Before we get closer to the entrance, I stop Joshua and look at him straight ahead, he turns his back to the mansion and I take his face lovingly, he is taller than me, so the gesture helps me to observe the roof of the place without looking suspicious, it is deserted, submerged in the night.

"Very smart," he says, stroking my cheek. I smile and look down as if I were blushing, I bring my lips to his and murmur:

"It's clean" then I kiss him gently. I don't know if Estirge is seeing us, but it is up to him to understand that it is for the safety of all of us, as well as the effectiveness of this plan.

On each side of the majestic mahogany door there are ten officers, they wear black suits, they look like guests, but they are not. In Toot they copied that trend from SyanL. In social events, uniforms are not allowed in the special guards, as they interfere with the expected elegance. It is stupid and very impractical, but even so, it is something that is customary to do in my country.

As we approach the entrance, I see how Dora takes care of greeting everyone who recognizes her, there are recording cameras and photographic units everywhere; the press is invited only to witness the arrival of those attending the Gala, but they cannot enter. Dora takes advantage and poses for each camera, she does it with Satiro by her side.

"Who is the gentleman, Miss Tarin?" Shouts a reporter wearing a neat tuxedo, since the rule of elegance also applies to the media.

"My fiancé!" She replies, but she doesn't stop. I don't know in which moment Ramón de Barbe's niece took it for granted that she and Sátiro were engaged. As we move forward a nervous knot weighs on my chest, but I restrain it with wide smiles and silly little jokes like any silly heiress would in my place.

When we get to the part where the guards are with *scanntubes* to check the absence of weapons or explosives on the guests, I start to have a bad feeling.

Dora delivers her invitation.

"Are they all with you tonight, Miss Tarin?" Asks one of them, checking the invitation.

"Yes, is there a problem?" She answers, with the same arrogant voice we heard at the hotel reception.

"Not at all," he answers, smiling.

"Perfect," Dora's voice softens.

"I'll only need your IDs," he explains with a friendly smile, "they will be returned to you at the end of the event."

"What?" Dora questions, raising her voice, astonished, "but, what do you think my friends and my fiancé are?" she remarks, "Criminals? murderers? Wasn't it clear that they are with me?"

"Miss, I beg you, it's for safety reasons."

"No problem, my love," Satiro begins, so as not to arouse suspicion in the guards.

"Of course there is a problem!" She says, it would be preferable if they didn't ask us for anything, but neither should a scandal be convenient for us, nor attract the attention of those in charge. Fortunately, one of our objectives for the night is precisely who appears in that moment. Among a crowd of bodyguards, dressed in outstanding white, arrives Alex Zendejas, who also wears a pearl-colored suit, but very elegant, as if he were on his way to a ceremony in front of the sea of La Costa.

"But it is Dora Tarín herself!" He exclaims, approaching Dora with open arms.

"I can't believe the years that have passed without seeing you!" She replies, forgetting about the guards and merging into a hug with the newcomer. For the first time all night she lets go of Satiro's hand. It doesn't seem like he cares at all, he even discreetly wipes the sweat from his palm inside his suit pocket.

"You're shining, Alex!" Dora says and it's true, I must admit, Alex Zendejas is in many ways impressive. It is not his height, nor his beautiful face, but an expression of arrogance and rebellion at the same time.

"I'm not the only one," he answers, I realize that his gaze falls on Silfide, this time Satiro's gesture goes darken.

"Oh, no, no, no," Dora intervenes, pulling Silfide by the hand, my friend's face seems to indicate that by accident she took the body of a dead mouse when looking for something in the cupboard, "This lady has a partner!" she says and then lets go of her as if it were her pet, pushing her towards Estirge. Silfide takes a breath with extreme patience.

"Ah, too bad!" Alex responds, who immediately changes the subject, "by the way, what are you guys doing here at the door? Why don't you come in?" he asks looking at us. His eyes linger on me for a moment "you look familiar, I'm sure I've seen you before," he says. The knot in my chest turns to steel and my mind races to that recording of the airport. Alex Zendejas is a very important businessman in Toot, he is surely aware of that incident. I try to smile, Joshua lets go of my hand, discreetly, maybe ready to fight if necessary, I see that the rest of my teammates also take a simple attack position that goes unnoticed.

"Me?" My smile breaks as does my voice, "I don't think so, I would remember you," I say, trying to express all the flirtation that my nerves allow me.

"I'm sure I know you," he insists. "Didn't we get drunk on cheap Whiskey from the coast at Patthy Luy's party last summer?" He asks, narrowing his eyes. I can almost hear a sigh of relief from inside everyone else.

"Oh no!" Dora intervenes, she does not like to be left out of any conversation, that is clear, "she can't be friends with Patthy!", she goes to Alex, "you know how selective

Luys are at their parties" the stupid prat comments. What is that supposed to mean?

"Why are we still here in the cold when we could be inside, drinking a good glass of whiskey?" Alex says, the night breeze blowing his messy hair. A detail strikes me suddenly. He comes alone, no one accompanies him, no one hangs on that arm that we surely know is one of the most desired in Toot, and perhaps even in SyanL. If there is something for which I am necessary in this group, it is because of the extreme attention that I dedicate to details, whether they are minimal and imperceptible, I do not let them go and in it, I see two important ones: a ring on the angular finger and a glimpse of sadness in emerald eyes. My mind quickly analyzes previously studied information about Alex and how it matches the observed details. Dora's voice explaining that the guards have offended us by asking for identification distracts me.

"Let them in," Alex tells the main guard.

"Mr. Zendejas, the protocol…"

"My friend." Alex lowers his voice, but I can clearly hear what he says "the protocol is for assholes", he ends, the guard doesn't say anything else.

The Gala is full with people and the orchestra plays in the back of the first floor, a pianist stands out, his skin tone, tanned as a walnut, and is his instrument that is heard the most. In the room where we have been led, people are pacing from one place to another. The dresses, mostly black, are worn by tall, pretty, blonde women, no one stands out, they all look like serial dolls, as if they were designed to be here. However, the same does not happen with the male sex, since almost all the guests are men between fifty and sixty years old, all elegantly dressed, impeccable in their manners and demeanor, the contrast with the twentysomethings that accompany them is extreme. Joshua, Estirge, Drider and Sátiro do stand out for their youth and masculinity, yet none of the women seem to take them into account,

"Let's take a picture!" Suggests Ondina, preparing his Nexus. We pose for the photograph, but we know that she is doing a quick scan of the entire room, which will be sent to Reneé instantly. "Excellent!" She says, analyzing the photo.

"I'll see you later," informs Alex Zendejas, "I have to go greet some customers," he smiles politely and walks away. Guilt hits me. That young businessman, with a ring on his finger and an air of nostalgia in his eyes, will not live beyond tonight. I don't like this feeling; guilt always leads to fear. I don't know Alex, I've never seen him in my life, he's not my friend, he's not even a SyanL citizen. On the contrary, he is a spoiled child of the rival nation. I don't have to feel for any condescension.

"Gorgona?" Drider leans closer, interrupting my thinking. He looks at me, there is a dark depth in his eyes. He has always breathed that kind of darkness, I know it is not the gray suit he wears, nor his wavy hair, held and orderly. It's something more.

"Yes?" I answer, returning a bit to reality. This exaggerated formality is due to that awkward kiss that night. The rest of my classmates roam the room. Estirge and Silfide dance to the rhythm of the piano, mingling with the rest of the people.

"Go away," he says, his eyes looking so threatening as if the enemy had always been me. However, I know what he means, I look away in annoyance.

"Again the same thing?" I ask and try to get away, he takes my arm but hides the strength of it very well.

"Shall we dance?" He asks, without waiting for an answer, he takes me by the waist. I don't want to, I don't like the attitude he's taken lately, but I agree, "Yes, the same again, and this is the second time I do it, probably that's enough," he says, I laugh slyly. Drider has always been the top representative of *last times*:

"This is the last time you call me in the middle of the night to get you out of a systems mess," He had said to Satiro.

"Never again will you bother me with such easy and ridiculous substances, Ondina, if you have doubts, call another idiot,"

"This is the last time you ask me for a favor"

"It is the last time I step on the cemetery "

"I will never inquire about it again"

"I don't understand your laugh," he says, "I didn't say something funny."

"It's nothing, I'm nervous."

"Well, relax then," he asks, I feel his clear gaze scrutinizing me "and listen to me: you know perfectly well that you can trust me, fully and you know the reason very well" he indicates as if he was scolding me, this seems anything but a declaration of love, his voice has that bell of command, of arrogance that has always had, "I love you."

"Drider," I reply, for some reason, the hollow of my stomach is far from pleasant.

"Let me say it, at least let me do it," he begs, out of the corner of my eye, I see Estirge still dancing with Silfide, "we are just a few minutes away from starting the plan, Lola should be here soon, and Corina, you are the most important friend that I have, you accused me of betraying you, of not protecting your Nexus"

"Sorry," I mutter, it makes me feel guilty, but I don't look down.

"Years ago, when my parents were killed, you saw me disappear from the face of the earth and you did not lift a finger to locate me, for a message, a call, a letter. You were not there for me."

"That's not fair," I answer, although he is totally right, but it bothers me to hear it, it hurts to be reminded of how you made a mistake.

"What's not fair? Turn your back on me? Relegate me?" His gaze falls on Estirge, who also turns to us, they both look at each other and I wish I was somewhere else, far from here.

"Drider, this is not the right time," I tell him, forcing him to look at me.

"We don't know if there will be more time. And you never listen, you don't understand that you should run away from here, run away ..."

"I'm not going to run away," I answer, he seems to have been left speechless. People begin to perceive a certain emotion, Lola is about to arrive.

"You are the only person to whom I would always give another chance" Drider's voice is cold, as always, "and that chance, is asking you to go now, go and save your life," I look at him sadly, "I know you weren't there when I needed you , but I want you to be in the future," his gaze restrains a little to the usual coldness.

"Drider," I say, letting go of his hands little by little, separating myself from him, "even if I survive all this," I look at Estirge, I see him approaching us, alone, "even if I don't die today," I continue and what I'm about to say hurts, but I want to be honest, "I won't be by your side in the future," I conclude and feel Estirge's hand entwining mine, my voice trembles and guilt begins to eat into my insides, "I'm sorry," I manage to say with a small voice , trying to avoid crying to impossible levels.

Estirge says nothing, he holds my hand, impassive and understanding, letting me choose. He knows that I have chosen him, that I would do it over and over again, regardless of anything.

"I understand," says Drider, "I finally understand," he remarks, he is about to move away when our Nexus vibrate at the same time, it is Joshua's indication, Lola is about to enter.

252

CHAPTER

46

I locate my mates visually. We place ourselves in the positions that Joshua has indicated to us. The room lowers its lights and leaves us in a dim gray color. A blue light points at the door, Ramón approaches the illuminated spot and the rest of the guests open the way, it seems like a mechanical rehearsal choreography, as everything is in this country: mechanical, cold, hard.

The front doors open and there she is: Lola Tehran, her platinum hair glued to her head, glows as if it will reflect the moon and not the light that illuminates the room. Everyone present applauds and she thanks them with smiles. Ramón approaches her and embraces her politely. Lola's heavy body wears a long black dress, with blue ruffles, Toot colors. Ramón presses a button on his Nexus and speaks through it without raising the volume, his voice fills the space thanks to the device.

"Friends and citizens of Toot, our efficient nation; with a pleasure that surpasses me, I welcome to my humble enclosure our President, Dr. Lola Teheran, who with her fine presence, ennobles this gala organized by the De Barbé family" with his arm he points to the people on his right, the family, there is Dora Tarín, this has been the only moment in which she has detached herself from Sátiro, "President…" Ramón addresses Lola, "it is an honor and a pleasure that you are here with us in this simple and humble ceremony."

"Now she'll introduce herself," Joshua murmurs to Estirge. He's right, Lola, almost like coming out of a script, gives her greeting speech.

"Dear citizens," she begins, her voice is sour and thick, like her appearance, "I am happy of being here, accompanying Ramón and you, the most hard-working and elevated citizens of the planet," she smiles, "later I will inform you of some important matters, for now I just want to thank Ramón and his family," she says, a loud applause breaks out in the place. I see Estirge approach Joshua, muttering something. I observe Lola without losing detail, next to her is Luis Romano, dressed completely in black, he has no visible weapons, but he must carry them somewhere in his suit. Alex Zendejas also approaches and kisses Lola, she returns a quick kiss on the lips and I see how the President kisses Ramón in the same way. At the moment the four of them are together, but there are many people surrounding them, we will have to follow the plan and stick to it,

Satiro and Drider discreetly approach the stairs.

"Come," Estirge's voice takes me out of concentration. I feel his hand grip my arm, he's cold, he must be as nervous as I am.

"Where?" I ask, his eyes are transparent despite the dark brown in them, contrast of twilight city, as is SyanL. He smiles at me and I trust everything he does. He takes my hand, and we walk among the people, but it is as if all these guests do not exist. My gaze meets Silfide´s, who also smiles the same, with the confidence of a life, with the eternal, clean and pure friendship of someone who is like you, someone who has been wrong as you have done, who has hurt in the same way and understands you. I don't want to die; I don't want anyone to die.

Estirge and I came down a long corridor, with stairs to the second floor that can't be seen. In the Gala room there are stairs that connect to the second floor and in the corridor next to the entrance as well, my friends will go up that corridor when the moment is right. Under the stairs where we approach in this lonely part of the house is a small room that serves as a cellar, as Joshua explained to us. So I guess: he wants to be with me alone, as if it were a farewell, to be by my side before facing the danger that awaits us a few minutes away. I don't think anymore, I hug him and finally kiss him as freely as possible. I feel his face in my hands, and I think that without a doubt, this would be the best moment to leave the world. He separates and I see his eyes a few millimeters away, I feel him shaking but I'm not sure if it's for the moment or because of fear.

"Come on, we still have a few minutes," he suggests and leads me to the door under the stairs, my heart beating fast.

"How did you get the key?" I ask him, he smiles and winks at me.

"You forget that I can do everything" he says, opens the door and I enter.

Then I hear the noise that makes me understand instantly. I turn almost immediately, but it is late: Estirge closed the door behind me, he did not enter with me.

"What? What are you doing, Estirge?" I question, desperate, "No! Please! Open the door!" I try, but I can't raise my voice, I can't scream risking to get someone's attention, "open the door, Estirge!" I say to the closed door, "Don't do this!" I hate this door, this hard wood like a coffin "Jimmy, please!", the fear invades me, the fear of losing him, the fear that has always followed us, the fear of a hospital, a funeral home, a cemetery, an empty church, f calls at midnight, of bad news, everything invades my body and through the tears I can only make out the door, "Why?" I ask at last, giving up, my voice is already broken by crying, his on the contrary is clear and serene.

"Saying *I love you* is easy when you have the right ... I don't now, I don't know, but I can't lose you," he says. I hear his footsteps moving away, no, I don't want him to die either, I can't allow it. I take out my Nexus and dial Joshua's number.

"Yes?" He answers, I feel a tremendous relief when listening to him, behind he distinguishes music and other voices.

"Joshua? Estirge locked me up, he left me in the cellar under the stairs of the north corridor, you have to-"

"I'm sorry, no," he answers.

"What? You must help me! Get me out of here! I'm part of the plan!"

"No Gorgona, you are not," he rectifies and hangs up. What did he mean by that? I dial Silfide's number but there is no answer, I want to die, I can't believe it. The Nexus trembles between my fingers. Drider, he must get me out of here. I dial and there is no answer, I hate this device. Satiro, come on… come on! Answer! ... nothing! I breathe deeply, I need to calm down, stabilize my ideas. She is my last hope. I press her name on my Nexus.

"Yes?" she says, finally!

"Ondina? Ondina, get me out of here, please get me out of here!"

"Where are you?"

"Estirge locked me in the cellar of the stairs, please, you have to help me.

"Calm down, which staircase?" she says, music is still being heard, but at that moment she stops talking I manage to perceive Ramón's amplified voice, Lola's speech must be about to start.

"Norte, in the north corridor, please help me."

"I'm going there," she hangs up. I pray internally that it is true, that she has a tiny light of our friendship on her heart and takes me out of here.

It's been a minute and a half when I hear a knock on the door.

"Gorgona?" I stick to the door as if the very voice of Ondina was going to transport me out of this space.

"Yes, yes, it's me, here I am, open me please."

"I don't have a key, but give me a minute," she says, inside me I appreciate that there is still some affection in it for me.

"Yes, sure, yes, but please hurry."

"Calm down, the others are already on the second floor, hidden, Silfide is watching the stairs, you and I will go up to the second floor when they are ready, as planned."

"Hurry up, please," I rush her, listening to the noises she makes when picking the lock. The door finally opens.

"Thank you! Thank you very much, Ondina!" I go out and walk next to her, Lola's speech is a few seconds away from starting. We mingle with the guests.

"We will go up the stairs to the left, which is where Silfide is, if everything goes well, you will not need to use any weapon" she explains referring to the fact that I was unable of picking up my gun, I am still nervous, I am completely confused. On the second floor balcony, looking down is Lola, to his left Romano and to his right Ramón de Barbe, next to him, Alex smiles openly.

"Please all stand in position for the national anthem of Toot," Luis Romano orders with his powerful voice, everyone raises their left arm with a closed fist until it is at the level of their own cheeks, it indicates strength and martiality, it is Toot's military salute. Ondina and I do it too as we glide among the guests, absentmindedly singing along with everyone the anthem of this country.

"Toot, blue-black nation, economy, militia and power!

Toot, the complete nation goes, to the top, to knowledge!

Toot, blue-black nation of cold fields, deep lakes

and brown mountains at sunset!

Toot independent, growing nation, economy, wisdom, and power!"

The general singing ends and the guests lower their arms.

"We will listen respectfully to the words of Dr. Lola Teheran, President of the free and independent nation of

Toot," Luis Romano's voice precedes applause in bulk, which Lola silences with a single hand gesture.

"Dear citizens, it is a great honor for me to be able to attend the gala offered tonight by my friend and faithful worker, Ramón de Barbé, who, as we all know, is the Director of Communication of our country, as well as the head of *InterToot*, our network cybernetics, where I am now a partner," Lola points at him smiling, the audience applauds although with less enthusiasm. I see among the people that Dora looks for Satiro with her eyes, she is anguished and desperate. Lola ends the applause for Ramón with the same gesture and the room is silent again, "I also thank Captain Luis Romano, my personal guard and Security Executor of the Nation of Toot," Luis does not smile, he just bows his head, not towards people, but towards Lola herself. The slight applause is drowned out by the presidential hand, "last, but not least, my eternal gratitude and love, to the elegant and helpful Alex Zendejas, director of Finance and Economy of our country, who is also accompanying us on this beautiful evening," she completes. Alex smiles and greets the guests. His popularity is noticeable for miles; this time Lola has to make a second gesture with her hand to get the audience to calm down.

Once the room grants her the silence that she requires to speak, she does not start suddenly, but runs a hand through her straight silver hair, a characteristic gesture of the president, and opens both arms, imitating a messianic pose, which of course is far from describing someone like her.

"My dear fellow nationals, as I have previously expressed, a satisfaction as pure as our whiskey invades me, being here, tonight, presiding," remarks, Ramón looks at her and widens his smile, evidently feigned, "this gala that is so important for Ramón , and I take the opportunity he gives me to communicate various issues" she clears her throat and presses a button on her Nexus, from which a hologram-like graphic is projected, framed in blue and black.

"These are our numbers," she continues, "as far as Whiskey production is concerned in the current two-month period of work," her gesture darkens for a second, "unfortunately, despite the fact that our production increased" she presses another button and the graph is projected, "Our sales and numbers are still below SyanL," she says annoyed, I can't help but smile, I look down and keep walking with Ondina among the guests, "LaGem and Kaoy keep importing *Joan Megghia* Whiskey in the first place as well as others from SyanL, leaving *Asia Roost*, our best brand in an embarrassing place number twelve!" she exclaims, "Twelve!" a murmur of indignation arises from the crowd. I don't know why they are surprised, those are not bad numbers for them, especially after having been twenty-three for more than fifty years.

"This situation," indicates Lola and turns off the projection "has to end. We are not trying hard enough," her lips, as silver as her hair, are moving with speed, "I am aware that this is a party, but we are people of Toot, we cannot allow ourselves too long without thinking about what is in our best interests concerns" the murmur of the guests is now of approval, "we will not allow SyanL to have superiority!" she exclaims, a loud applause now comes from the people gathered, the moment is near, Lola is about to finish her speech, "SyanL is a nation of vain bums who think their looks or talents will give everything to them! Delonge is nothing more than an attractive model, a frustrated musician, all he does is follow like a lamb the suggestions of the damn Reneé Lobo!" There is a lot of hatred in the voice of the President, it does not seem a contempt of nations, but something personal, I distinguish Silfide on the stairs. Ondina stands to one side to let me pass, she's doing well, she does have a hidden weapon and will watch my back.

"SyanL is a nest of rats!" Lola continues enraged, "A damn town with unserved luck!" she mentions excitedly. Then it happens, it is Joshua who takes Lola from behind, pointing a goldgun500 at her temple, Estirge does the same with Alex and Sátiro with Ramón, whose face is pure fear. Drider threatens the last of Toot's leaders, Luis Romano. The guests howl in anguish and surprise. I can see Toot's guards in the crowd, pointing at them, but my friends have the upper hand, one move and their President dies right here, before their eyes. The guards know it, but they still don't lower their weapons.

"We won't hurt anyone!" Joshua yells, "we're here for them and nobody else", he clarifies, we are close to Silfide, she doesn't look at us, she points to the audience, to anyone who makes the attempt to climb, "Don't risk yourselves," Joshua insists, "we only came for them!" he shouts. Then I see Lola's silver smile, a smile that reminds me of someone, but I can't remember clearly, because the words that come out of her mouth terrify me.

"I don't think so, darling," she says, those were the words expected by Luis Romano who with frenzied speed turns around and in a second, in a terrible second that I will never be able to forget, stabs Drider into the thorax. His gaze is lost and it will never return.

"No!" I yell, and I regret it, but my voice is covered by the noise of the rest of the people when the shots start.

The only thing I think about is the ridiculousness of my legs, not advancing at the speed I would like, he cannot be dead, Drider cannot be dead. I see how a handful of guards manage to threaten my friends in the midst of the confusion that has formed. It terrifies me to see how a guard holds Estirge and two of them have come to take Silfide away, she manages to shoot one of them, but the other holds her tightly.

"Ondina!" I turn my face, looking for her among the people, she is approaching me, on the second floor the guards are taking my friends, we must hurry, we must save them, "Ondina, come on!" I insist, however she sees me She looks at me as if I were a dying woman in a hospital bed. "Ondina, are you okay?" I take her by the shoulders. "We must help them! Now!", her eyes keep looking at me and surprisingly, she hugs me.

"What happen? You're ok?"

"I have never been better," when she separates, I don't see a tearful face, but her hands pointing to my face, the goldgun in her hands is identical to mine, she smiles and talks, "and this time I am not imitating you, Gorgona, this time I am the one who marks the difference, this time you are the second girl, this time you are the secondary character, this time ..." the resentment in her voice is almost obvious, as if that had been her tone since I met her in that office, looking for her lost brother in the SyanL archives, "this time the protagonist is me" completes, I look askance, there is no one around who can help me, people run and push, desperate to get out, I look into her eyes, in them I see that she is going to kill me, her look says that she is capable of doing it, she has already killed before, that is not a problem for her, but ...

"Why?" I ask, in my head there are many images, Drider dropping dead, the blood flowing from his body, the kiss I shared with Estirge not more than half an hour ago, Lola's speech, the faces of my parents, of my brothers, disappeared so many years ago.

I'm going to die.

"There is no answer to that, at least not a single one" she explains "I will let you imagine it, I want that you finally leave this fucking world without knowing it, so can you imagine it? didn't you always show it off? Your imagination? Your ideas?"

"We were friends."

"We were accomplices", she corrects and brings the weapon closer to my face, "us, the *Animalium* would have been better without you, Jimmy would have been better without you!"

"Don't call him by his name," I spit with all the hatred I can.

"I call him whatever the fuck I want! And you will no longer be there to do anything about it! I would happily kill you right now, but my part of the deal is to take you to Lola."

"What?" I ask, incredulous, "Lola?"

"I'm not the only one who wants your head, although believe me that Lola does not want it as much as I do, however it is she who has the power, walk!" she orders me.

Ondina works for Lola, for Toot, how come Delonge didn't notice? Or Reneé? How? I feel the goldgun on the back of my neck as she leads me to a room on the second floor, I can't risk it, if I try to disarm her, she will kill me, Ondina may be a bitch, but she is skilled.

"Move!" she says, kicking a door while still pointing at me. Inside, standing and holding, is each of my friends, except Drider, who lies at Lola's feet. The single image makes me want to vomit and makes me dizzy. In front of them, standing, Alex, Ramón and Luis, who in turn, point different weapons at them.

"No!" shouts Estirge when he sees me, "No!" he looks at Lola, desperate, "That was not the deal! Corina should come out unharmed, let her go!", he says again I'm there, not understanding at all.

"Excuse me," she answers, confused and amused at the same time "as you can see, it is not me who has her threatened and held, it is not me or any of my guards," Lola raises her hands innocently, everything becomes weirder.

"You are a traitorous bitch," Mumbles Silfide, looking at Ondina, who doesn't stop pointing at me "Shitty envious bitch!!" my friend says, Silfide's guard holds her tighter, Lola laughs and goes to Estirge.

"The truth is that, I don't know why Ondina agreed to work for me and give me your beloved Gorgona" she looks at him and approaches him, for a moment I think she will attack him, but she caresses his cheek tenderly, "I think she is also in love of you, darling" then he looks at me, his deep brown eyes fixed on me and before I realize, I understand everything, I remember the words spoken by Estirge several times: *my father's secret is something that I cannot take away, even if I wanted".*

"I must feel proud," continues Lola, "two beautiful girls in love with my son" confesses at last. Everyone looks at him in amazement, the only one who is unperturbed is Joshua, I've never seen him flinch.

"This was not the agreement we had!" Estirge yells at last.

"Don't yell at me, the SyanL manners your father taught you don't work on Toot," she orders, Ramón laughs.

My hands are tickling me, I didn't want anyone to die, but right now I want to crush all of them, Lola, Ramón, Luis Romano, Damn it! Drider is dead!

"And although I'm proud," Lola continues, with the gun in her hand she caresses Estirge's face, no, it can't be, she wouldn't, she wouldn't hurt him, she's his mother, "that you are such an attractive young man, so desired, brave and with so much passion," she looks at Ondina and then at me, her eyes, so similar to Jimmy's makes me swallow hard, I feel dizzy, the end is soon to come, I'm scared.

"I don't like that..." Lola continues, annoyed, "one of them is envious and traitorous!, it's a shame!" Lola smiles and points her gun at Ondina, who doesn't have time to react "Goodbye dear," Lola says just before shooting her. I stay paralyzed for a moment, then I try to take her weapon "Freeze!" Lola indicates, I raise my hands above my head and I look at her, then my gaze falls on Ondina, I see her, and although her eyes are still open, I know that she is dead. There is no blood spilled, Lola's shot is from a total expert, but that is not what catches my attention, it is not the absence of blood, but the presence of a word on Ondina's arm, a tattoo that I never seen before: *Diego*. I gulp, Lola laughs and continues her conversation with Estirge, still pointing at me.

"I thank you, son, you have given me the necessary elements to show the Peace World Congress, the piece of shit that Delonge. You, my beautiful son, have brought these shits to me, and that is more than I could ask…it is more than which I could ever have asked from your father" Lola's eyes look into a past that is far way, a past not in Toot, but in SyanL, "that weak man, with his mediocre job in the Joan Megghia company.." she laughs" he expected for me to stay there, in that bricky Sy4 place to see how my life would rotten", she explains, "can you imagine?" she looks at Estirge and caresses his face, like wondering how his childhood years were, those that she missed, "If I had stayed with your father, today I wouldn't be the president of a country!, I would be the rotter widow without any other wish that drinking a glass of whisky every once in a while, and that in the cae of have escaped unscathed to the crime that reigns in SyanL," Lola approaches Sátiro, posing her face to millimeters, " We know it is a nest of rats and gangsters, right? You know it from experience, dear, your brother was one of them," she says while giving him a quick kiss on the lips. Silfide moves in her place, wanting to shake off the tall, dark guard holding her. The struggle draws Lola's attention, "what a misfortune to live in SyanL," she continues, turning now to my friend, "amidst the garbage and loneliness," she says, staring at her, "But!" she laughs, with her arms she covers the entire office, "now I am here, with my people!" she points to Ramón, Alex and Luis, "it is a pity, my love" she tells her son, "that you were born in SyanL, and it is even worse that your useless father raised you" confesses Lola, "but everything will be different now," she turns around and I see that her weapon is aimed at me. She smiles and I don't want that her face is the last image in my head before I die, so I turn my eyes to Jimmy, his face in my mind is the only thing I want to take away from this earth.

"No!" he yells, hitting the guard that holds him, Lola backs away and Luis Romano protects her, I take advantage of the bewilderment to take the weapon from Ondina's inert hands, without thinking, I shoot at Romano, before he can attack Estirge, I keep holding the weapon and I see how Satiro and Silfide have thrown their respective guards out of control.

"Ramón!" Lola shouts, he tries to stop Sátiro, but Joshua shoots him and Ramón de Barbé's heavy body falls dead, his blood covers the neatness of his own home. Alex is the only one who is still standing, next to Lola, they both point towards my friends, who do not move anymore, they know: a move and both Alex and Lola will shoot without mercy. My shaking hand holds the gun, pointed at Lola, her lips no longer silver, but red, stained with splattered blood. Her weapon is not aimed at me, not at Satiro, Silfide or Joshua, but at him: Jimmy, his own son.

"I'm not surprised!" Lola shouts, hysterical, breaking the momentarily recovered calm, Jimmy breathes fiercely, also pointing at her, "whiskey producers, alcohol, you hinder people because you like to do it, you are violent by nature,"

Lola's gaze runs through us and his brown eyes project hatred and resentment, like her words.

"No," I say, almost in a whisper and I remember my grandfather, drinking his afternoon whiskey with Dad, I remember him in his green chair, with his tired feet and a pride that I was too young to understand, a pride about his country, pride of the tranquility of having worked a whole day, without harming anyone, "alcohol does not generate violence," I keep raising my voice, "whiskey does not generate it, in any case, it emboldens you to take out everything that you carry inside, as in you, President" I say, but I don't understand myself, I don't know what the meaning of my answer is.

"Typical rich girl from SyanL," she replies, "defending the indefensible, advocating a vice that your country is dedicated to motivate" she exclaims and looks at her son, "is this the person who has made you fall in love? This one, an upper-class orphan who-"

"I'm not an orphan!" I hold the goldgun dominating the shaking of my hand, "my family...they are not dead ..." I whisper with a barely audible voice.

"Oh, but they are," she answers, lowering the gun, I don't know why she does it, "just like Jair's brother is, or Jimmy's father," she says, smiling, "just like Adolfo's parents are and well..." she points to him, on the floor, dead for several minutes, "just as himself is now!" she laughs, without letting go of her weapon and looks at me approaching, I don't put down my goldgun, I don't trust her.

"Do you know what it was that always surprised me? Your little emotional conflicts," she looks at Estirge with shame, "and that includes you, my son, so jealous of Adolfo, of the love he always showed for this girl," she looks at me with contempt, "and that is something that you, and I mean *all of you*, do not understand: the sum of two solitudes or three or four, is not friendship, it is not love, either, but an even greater solitude, the duel you have lived through all your lives brings chaos and uncertainty, which is what you have become," Lola looks at me and with that harshness, she challenges me, "you will never shoot me, you would not dare to kill the only family that Jimmy has" she says with certainty, I feel cold tears sliding down both cheeks, I feel hopelessness and for a moment I have the desire that my family is dead, that I no longer live with this uncertainty, with this eternal doubt, I give up.

I slowly lower the gun and through the tears I see how Lola raises it and aims at me, it is too late, when the bullet penetrates my body I feel as if my flesh is burning, just for a second, then I fall to the ground and I have no control over nothing, not my legs, not my hands, not my life. Please, let the goodbye does not hurt so much, please, that it does not hurt so much.

ESTIRGE

Were lying on the shadow of your family tree

Your haunted heart and me

Tv on the radio.

Everything happens very fast, maybe it will be the last time things happen at this speed, without her, without Corina, I know that my life will be slow, it will have the calm that there is in the depths of any abandoned ocean.

Alex Zendejas was the one who should kill her, that was the plan, our last alibi. I see him raise his armed arm to end the life of Lola TehEran once and for all, but my anger is greater, my scream equates the sound of my weapon, of the golden bullet, colored like an ice painted whiskey that penetrates the head of my mother. I drop the goldgun and fall to my knees too. The alarm goes off: the President of Toot is dead.

"It's time!" shouts Alex, "go!, the jet is waiting for you!" I feel Joshua and Satiro's hands try to get me up, Silfide picks up a couple of silverguns while tears drip from her face. I don't want to go, I don't want a body, I don't want anything.

"Estirge!" Joshua picks me up, "leave her, she wanted you to live. Do you understand? Her greatest fear was seeing you dead," I let Joshua guide me to the balcony, the noise of the jet pierces me in the worst of my nightmares.

"Tell mom that I will communicate soon, we have won," I manage to hear Alex's words to Joshua, but I do not give it importance, I do not understand, my eyes can't be apart from Corina, who lies on the ground, a couple of feet away from me. The weakness comes to me suddenly and once on the plane, I cry in silence, wallowing in the solitude that will accompany me the rest of my days.

***

About the trial, I remember few things and only in isolated parts: Daniel Delonge's gray suit, the sobriety of the courtroom where it took place. It was a private trial, like many that take place at SyanL. Daniel and Reneé in front of me, next to me the Prosecutor of the World Peace Council, and in another section, Alex Zendejas declaring in my favor.

"Jimmy Atkint Teheran, innocent," the Prosecutor looks at me with a smile, not for me, not for my purchased freedom, not for anything that relates to the rest of us. Surely he will soon forget our faces. He has no reason to remember them. Daniel Delonge and Reneé have awarded him shares of stock in Joan Megghia, this in exchange for declaring our innocence. I bow my head slightly and let him continue, "Dulce Corr Yanz," he looks at Silfide who dressed completely in black, like me, nods.

"Innocent," he says, she smiles and the Prosecutor winks at her. I am disgusted by this decrepit old man and I am disgusted to be part of his corruption "Jair Abella Tatchert," looks at Satiro, who in turn, awaits a verdict that we all know, "innocent."

"Thank you very much Prosecutor Ioshima," Reneé speaks with his usual authority. The prosecutor grins.

"There is nothing to be grateful for, on behalf of the World Council of Peace, I appreciate your hospitality, President Delonge, Executor," he makes a slight inclination, eager to review the amounts of the shares that have been granted, "President Alex Zendejas, we appreciate your collaboration in this court, I wish you the best of luck and success in your occupancy in the prosperous nation of Toot."

"Prosecutor, I am flattered," Alex replies, "I remind you of my invitation for the audits that are necessary in my country," he concludes.

"Thanks Prosecutor, that's all," Reneé cuts, before the Prosecutor continues with his flattery. He seems to get the message and leaves the place, taking his new shares with him.

"I'd like to have a private conversation, if you don't mind, Alex," Delonge says. The new President of Toot smiles broadly.

"This way," Reneé indicates, pointing the way to Daniel Delonge's office that connects to the living room. The three enter through a door after typing a password and it is Reneé who turns towards us momentarily, as if remembering that we are still here.

"There is someone who wishes to speak with you, wait here" she orders and enters the office, following Delonge and Zendejas. Through the door where Prosecutor Ioshima went out, Joshua enters, dressed in a dark blue suit, his hair now cut short.

"Look who has deigned to appear," comments Satiro approaching,giving him a hug.

"I had unfinished business that couldn't wait," Joshua smiles.

"You have missed our trial," Silfide says, kissing him on the cheek.

"I'm sorry, but I've heard from Ioshima himself that there has only been room for a trio of angels."

"How come they didn't put you in a trial?" I ask, looking at him, somehow, it seems like it's the first time I've seen him.

"It's simple, my last name is Lobo," he reminds us. And it's true. He is Joshua Lobo, son of Reneé Lobo, he has never been to Toot more than to visit his brother, the new President of Toot, Alex Zendejas Lobo. His name does not appear in any file, he is not involved at all.

"It's funny," I say, "you proudly wear your motherly surname, something that I will never be able to do," I laugh reluctantly and I feel that everything hurts again. Joshua pats me on the back, and it's all I need to feel his solidarity.

"The reason why I'm here is an official matter," Joshua begins, speaking seriously, "Daniel Delonge has offered you a position in his government," he announces, " to the three of you. He wants you to be Deputy Chiefs of Security in the Official Cabinet of SyanL."

"Really? That can't be true," Silfide answers, incredulous.

"As true as I have your contracts right here," Joshua responds, pulling out a Nexpad, ready to receive our fingerprints.

"We are murderers" Satiro observes, "although Ioshima has kept his mouth shut in exchange for a handful of shares, that does not change the fact and Delonge knows it."

"Exactly, and it is precisely what he needs, what SyanL needs. Righteous murderers, disguised as corrupted politicians," he explains, "Delonge acknowledges that the master plan was merely designed by you, Jimmy. He knows that being a double agent with your own mother is something few people dare to do. You stood up for what you loved, Corina, and for what you respected, SyanL. You knew the risk of telling Lola that you would hand her over the Animalium to incriminate Delonge with the mere purpose of reaching her and gaining her trust ... those are bigger words that not even Reneé herself could have drawn," he says, looking into my eyes. Every one of his words hurts. Mentions of Corina and my mother hurt me.

"We have a file," Silfide begins, "a large file" Joshua shows her the document on the NexPad.

"Put your fingerprint here and consider that file deleted."

"What is Delonge looking for in return?" I ask at last. In SyanL nobody gives you anything just because, that has been clear to me, everything has a price.

"Nothing" Joshua responds, "there is only one condition," he says, "at the moment that your file is erased, *Satiro*, *Silfide* and *Estirge*, they die with it, we do not need them, we need Jair, Dulce and Jimmy."

***

Jair's voice awakens me suddenly. I rub my eyes heavily and although I am sleeping better, there are still moments of the day that weigh on me. Six in the afternoon is one of them.

"We're out," he announces to me through the Nexus.

"One second," I answer, standing up. I rub my eyes again and a blurry image in the mirror becomes clear: me.

I once read that people dress in black for mourning because their humor does not allow them to have the courage to choose a particular outfit. True, having a broken soul is enough to add absurd tribulations to it. The mirror matches and reflects the sadness of my suit. I walk to the glass cabinet and pick up a small, expensive 500-milliliter bottle of Joan Megghia. *Water of life*, for me it will never be that again. I pour myself the whiskey in a wide golden glass. When the taste of rain and wet wood fills my mouth, I feel like crying, but there are no tears. *Water of death*, yes that's more suitable. I put the bottle in the cabinet and leave my apartment. Jair, Dulce, and Joshua are waiting for me in the car.

"Ready?" He asks me once I sit next to him in the back seat.

"Here I am," I answer with the obvious gesture. He looks at me questioningly, I know what he means. I nod, lying. I will never be ready to say goodbye, even in a symbolic way, to the person who amazed me at being so virtuous, and who made me love as only an abandoned child loves.

"Reneé needs you to go to the Security and Execution Building tomorrow. She understands your situation, you don't have to stay for work yet, but she wants to introduce you to the staff," Jair tells me. I nod, his blue eyes questioning me in the rearview mirror.

"Delonge has said that you can take all the time you need," adds Dulce's voice.

"Tomorrow I will report to work," I announce, they look at each other. "I'm fine and the sooner the better," I say.

"Delonge said that ..." Dulce insists.

"Tomorrow I'll be there," I finish. Nobody else says a word and in a couple of minutes, we're at SyanL cemetery.

***

When Jair found me in this place, he did it by making fun of me, while I was arguing with my dead father, many years ago. Today they have left me only a few moments. I see them at the entrance to the cemetery, Jair holds Dulce's hand, both entertained in Joshua's conversation. I look at Corina's niche and speak like that time I said goodbye to my only family in this same place:

"Corina…there is no grave for you, only a niche with the ashes that were sent to us from Toot, the niche has a small snake in it, you know? You are not behind these doors so I can't yell at you, I can't curse you for leaving me, as I did with my father. Unlike him, you didn't leave me a secret, but an empty heart. It emptied when I saw you fall in front of my eyes. And then I started to divert my thoughts, as always, like when I thought of you and when I fell in love with you." I gulp to hold the tears and then I continue:

"I tend to evade things, like a fucking defense mechanism, unlike you, the most beautiful example I can give. Your way of showing what you wanted and the way you did it ... How amazing was to meet someone like you. I care about you more than you think and more than I could ever demonstrate, you were a wonderful person and I say it firmly, even though you are no longer there," I look at the snake in the niche, small, marked, like that hanging she used, showing her symbol.

"I remember the last time someone called me *Jimmy*, I always let everyone know that I don't like to be called that way. I still don't like it, I feel it very personal. But I never cared that you used to do it like that." I remember her voice saying my name with different feelings.

"Only like that I can get used to people calling me *Jimmy*, in that innocent way, not in another way. It was a *Hey, everything is fine ...* that's how I want it to sound, like you, because with you everything was fine, even the worst moments, even if we were bad people, everything next to you...was amazing"

The sky is clouding over and it hurts me to know that the weather now matches my feelings.

"Corina ... I know that you are fine, right? on another side of the universe, in another place that I cannot even imagine, but I know that you are, and that although nothing has been as we would have planned, I am here to say goodbye, but not as if not nothing would have happened, not without promising that I will come back here, to talk to you and feel that you listen to me, that you still see me."

***

I am a fool. I think about it as I open the door to my apartment. Being jealous of the fact that Adolfo's and Corina's niches are together is absurd even for me. I look out the window towards a SyanL that receives the first drops of rain from the station. Vehicles continue their march, people leave work, whiskeys are bought and drunk.

It's the sensible way to close a day or a cycle with a glass of whiskey. I turn to the cabinet as the afternoon progresses at a speed that seems to rush me.

A wave of chill runs through my body when I take the bottle in my hands, which I took before leaving for the cemetery. There, on the neck of it, is the hanging of the snake that Gorgona used. I feel it, put it close to my nose: it smells like whiskey. I'm dizzy, I don't understand. I take the goldgun out of my pocket, someone must have left the hanging. I register my department quickly.

No one.

The phone rings and it startles me.